BUCHI EMECHETA was born in Lagos, Nigeria. Her father, a railway worker, died when she was very young. At the age of 10 she won a scholarship to the Methodist Girls' High School, but by the time she was 17 she had left school, married and had a child. She accompanied her husband to London where he was a student. Aged 22, she finally left him, and took an honours degree in sociology while supporting her five children and writing in the early morning.

In the Ditch, her first book, was published in 1972. It was followed by *Second-Class Citizen*, *The Bride Price*, *The Slave Girl*, which was awarded the Jock Campbell Award, *The Joys of Motherhood*, *Destination Biafra*, *Naira Power*, *Double Yoke*, *Gwendolen*, *The Rape of Shavi* and *Kehinde*, as well as a number of children's books and a play, *A Kind of Marriage*, produced on BBC television. Her autobiography, *Head Above Water*, appeared in 1986 to much acclaim.

BUCHI EMECHETA

IN THE DITCH

Heinemann

Heinemann Educational Publishers
A Division of Heinemann Publishers (Oxford) Ltd
Halley Court, Jordan Hill, Oxford OX2 8EJ

Heinemann: A Division of Reed Publishing (USA) Inc.
361 Hanover Street, Portsmouth, NH 03801-3912, USA

Heinemann Educational Books (Nigeria) Ltd
PMB 5205, Ibadan
Heinemann Educational Boleswa
PO Box 10103, Village Post Office, Gaborone, Botswana

FLORENCE   PRAGUE   PARIS   MADRID
ATHENS   MELBOURNE   JOHANNESBURG
AUCKLAND   SINGAPORE   TOKYO
CHICAGO   SAO PAULO

British Library Cataloguing in Publication Data
A catalogue record for this book is available from the British Library.

ISBN 0435 90994 0

Cover design by Touchpaper
Cover illustration by Synthia Saint James

Phototypeset by Wilmaset Ltd, Birkenhead, Wirral
Printed and bound in Great Britain
by Cox & Wyman Ltd, Reading, Berkshire

94 95 96 97 10 9 8 7 6 5 4 3 2 1

CONTENTS

To the memory of my father
Jeremy Nwabudike Emecheta
Railwayman and 14th Army Soldier in Burma

1   *Qualifying for the Mansions*

There was a crik, and a crack, then another crik, then crack, crack, cra. . . . Adah pulled herself up with a start and sat in the hollow of the large double bed. It had a gradual valley-like hollow, which gave it a sort of U look. On both sides of her the mattress rose gently, just like two table-lands sheltering her in a hollow valley. The crik and the crack sounds came once more and she grabbed her four-month-old baby from its carry-cot. The cot was lying on one of the table-lands.

The sleepy baby was cross, her little face twisted in anger. Adah held the wet bundle to her breast and stared at her room-mate, the Great Rat. The rat was by now used to Adah's fright, he had long sensed that Adah was terrified of his sharp piercing eyes, long mouth and his big brown body. He stood there, relaxed but watchful, wondering what trick Adah was up to now.

She was always too scared to shout. Her mouth was dry and she was too frightened even to move. The rat got bored with watching her, started to hop from one table to another, happily enjoying its night play. Adah's eyes followed its movements in the dim candlelight, then carefully and noiselessly she stretched out to reach the small reading-table by the big bed, picked up one of the library books she had piled on the table, aimed carefully at the hopping rat, and flung. The rat, for once, was scared. It ran right into the broken wardrobe at the end of the room, disturbing a group of sleeping cockroaches. One of

1

the frightened cockroaches ran into Adah's hollow for maternal protection.

She had been told the week before that the Council would soon have them rehoused.

She put the baby back in her cot, but did not dare go to sleep again. She was happy in her victory over the rat; at least she might now get some peace for a few nights. Another crashing noise jarred into her happy thoughts from the outside. 'Oh, not *again*!' she moaned to herself, nearly in tears.

This time it was her landlord. He had long given her notice to quit the premises with her five young children. But unfortunately for Adah, she was black, separated from her husband, and, with five kids all under six, there were few landlords who would dream of taking the like of her into their houses.

Her landlord, a Nigerian, like herself, being aware of Adah's predicament, was, of course, taking the best advantage of the situation. The rent he charged was double what was normally asked for rooms in such houses. He now wanted her to leave because she had had the effrontery to ask him to do something about the rats, the cockroaches and the filth. When he had failed to do anything about them, she had been to the Town Hall and, because there was no other place for her to live just then, the Council had stepped in. They had asked the landlord to do some repairs, and even asked him to give Adah a rent-book.

To give Adah a rent-book would have put him in trouble because, being a council tenant, he had pretended to the authorities that Adah was a relative and only a guest. He had begged Adah to withdraw her application for a flat from the Council but it was too late. There were, however, still lots of things he could do to make her life miserable. He would thunder at her kids for any of the slightest childish noises; this happened so frequently that one of her boys would run at the sight of any black man, and she dared not leave them alone in

2

the flat for fear of what might happen to them. She could not leave any piece of food or drink in the filthy shared kitchen for fear of it being poisoned. All their food had to be kept under her bed, so it was hardly surprising that the number of rats had increased. The man was desperate and would stop at nothing. He had switched off the electricity so that she had to keep a candle burning all night, conscious of the terrible fire risk to the children, but even more afraid of what accidents could happen in utter darkness. But now there was something new: he was trying magic.

The poor man, instead of sleeping like everybody else, would wake up very early in the morning, round three or four, drape himself in colourful African material, just like juju masqueraders in Lagos, and start moving to and fro to the music of his low-toned mournful songs. When Adah had first seen this figure she could not believe her eyes. She was on the verge of screaming, but when she looked closer and saw it was only her landlord, she could feel only pity and contempt for him. Adah was more afraid of the rat than the juju landlord.

This morning she simply stared at him, not knowing what to do next; then, amused, she decided to join in his songs which, of course, she had known from childhood. Why was it that she was not afraid? she wondered. Was it because here in England one's mind was always taken up with worrying about the things that really matter? But juju mattered to her at home in Nigeria all right; there, such a scene in the middle of the night could even mean death for some. Probably, she thought, it was because there it was the custom, the norm, and what everybody believed in. The people not only believed in juju but such beliefs had become internalised and it would not occur to anyone to think otherwise. But here, in north-west London, how could she think of the little man who was so familiar to her by day in his greasy second-hand lounge suit as a medicine man? She had heard rumours, and read in the papers, of other Africans in London being 'terrorised' by juju. *But I am tough and free*, she thought, *free*, she repeated to herself. In England she was free to keep her job, keep her kids, do her studies; she felt safe to ignore the juju man and his pranks. No, the juju trick would not work in England, it was out of place, on alien ground. God dammit, juju, in England you're surrounded by walls of unbelief!

On that particular morning, the landlord had either slept late or was very tired, or both, for Adah soon heard the rattling of the milkman's van; it must be six a.m. Mrs Devlin, the Irish woman living in the top flat, padded down with her empty bottles rattling, the milkman came up the road with his merry whistle, and the landlord stood on the pavement, just outside Adah's ground-floor window, like a statue, apprehensive of the rattle and whistle. Adah watched from the window, fascinated. What would happen now? she wondered.

Mrs Devlin gave such a scream that the poor milkman had to lean against his van for support. The landlord could not push the old lady away, for she blocked the only doorway leading into the house. He simply did not know how to begin to explain what he had been doing, and stared at them all, his eyes looking so white in his black face. Adah did not want to miss the show, so, tying a *lappa* over her nightdress, went out. The landlord's wife also came out, and so did the other Nigerians living down the road. How could the landlord explain to this group of Londoners why, at such an early hour, he had tied a red cloth round his naked body and arranged an ostrich feather sticking up at the back of his head, looking to them like a television Red Indian who had had a shot too many?

The milkman fixed his gaze on him, silently demanding an explanation. The face of the landlady was another picture. It was still unmade-up and she still had her hair threaded (like many African women, she 'threaded' her hair before going to bed, in small plaits, so that when the thread was taken out, the hair would lie on the head in attractive coils and not stick out), and in her haste she had not remembered to cover it with her wig. Mrs Devlin, who was on good speaking terms and neighbourly with Adah, looked appealingly to her to explain.

4

Just then the landlady's face turned to her, saying without words, 'Please don't say anything, please don't.'

Adah started to stare at the ceiling by the doorway to avoid looking at any more faces. Then she thought of the picture they, the Nigerians, must present to their neighbours. The plaits on the landlady's head would definitely remind any foreign person of the pictures of black devils they knew from their childhoods, for her plaits stood out straight, just like four horns. The landlord with the feather looked like the Devil's servant. Adah too was part of the picture. Her *lappa* with yellow and red splashes provided a good background.

Blast these illustrators! Who told them that the Devil was black? Who told them that angels are always white? Had it never occurred to them that there might be black angels and a white devil?

The milkman recovered first from the shock. 'Were you going to *her* room?' he asked, deliberately, with accusation in every word, pointing at Adah's room.

Adah did nothing to help the landlord's dilemma but was quite regretting coming out in the first place. She did not know why she was so keen on keeping her landlord's secret. Patriotism? After all, one did not like to have one's dirty linen washed in public. Whatever happened, they were all originally from the same country, the same colour, both caught in the entangled web of an industrial society. He wanted to make money from his house to pay for his studies, Adah wanted the proper value for the rent she paid. In their own country, the situation would never have occurred in the first place. Igbo people seldom separate from their husbands after the birth of five children. But in England, anything could be tried, and even done. It's a free country.

The landlady started scolding her husband in Yoruba. The other Nigerians agreed with her. Why should he take it upon himself to frighten a lonely woman? Did he not fear God? The whole race of men were beasts. She had always said that, in fact her mother told her so at home when she was little. He had

5

made a fool of himself. God only knew what these whites were going to do.

To Adah she said nothing, but her frank speech was meant as an apology. It was very funny really, because everybody knew that everything the landlord had done had been planned by the two of them.

When the landlady started her speech in the Yoruba language, which Adah understood perfectly, the white people started to move away. The milkman swore, so did Mr Devlin and his two sons, who by now had joined the party. Mrs Devlin would go to the 'Town 'all, Monday'.

2 *Drifting to the Mansions*

After a cold and rainy night, the day was warm. It was early spring. Adah found a space on a bench beside two women who were talking about death, and sat down. It seemed very odd to be talking about death on such a beautiful afternoon, and in such a beautiful park. She looked at the two women momentarily and decided that the day was too fresh, too pure and too lovely to listen to death-talk.

The blue sky was liberally dotted with white clouds. The flats opposite had window-boxes displaying the first flowering shrubs. There were daffodils everywhere. Daffodils in the park, daffodils in the front and back gardens of houses, daffodils edging the park's footpaths, all planted with the type of carelessness that has a touch of calculation.

She inhaled the pure fresh air around her and said under her breath, 'I feel so happy I could burst.' A group of pigeons wobbled towards her as she unpacked her fish sandwich. She broke one slice of bread into pieces and threw it at them. They pecked at the crumbs agitatedly. Why was it that pigeons were always hungry? Eating as quickly as they did must give them stomach ache.

It was a Friday, and her half-day. She would have her sandwich and spend a couple of hours in the library, then she would cook, then what, she would clean the flat, then bed. Q.E.D.!

But the warmth of the sun was caressing and, after the sort of

7

nights she had been having lately, the lure to doze off was too much of a temptation. The last bit of resistance to sleep was removed when the two women talking about death decided to leave. So she could snore if she liked.

Africans say that it is possible to have four seasons in one day in England, and indeed when Adah woke it might have been any winter day. The park was empty, even the pigeons had taken shelter from the icy cold rain. She got up quickly, looked at the clock on the tower and realised that she had slept the two hours she had saved for reading. Not to worry . . . she had enough fresh air in her lungs to face her choky flat. She hurried home.

Mrs Devlin was at the door of their house when she got home. She was excitedly talking to her friend Mrs Marshall, who was, as usual, holding the lead of her black dog. The two women turned to look in Adah's direction when they saw her coming. She was sure they were still talking of the juju episode which had been so spiced to flavour that she was already the heroine of a rather dramatic story. But heroines, being human like everybody else, do get bored of being praised. Not being in the mood to listen to any more new versions of the juju episode, she decided to dash past them, without greeting, to the nursery.

'Hey, what do you think *you're* doing? Come 'ere, we've good news for yer.'

Adah wondered what good news there could be for her. She seldom got any news, but good news – well, she might as well listen.

'They've got a flat for yer. The manager was 'ere a minute ago, he said he would come back in thirty minutes to see if you were back.'

'Me? A council flat for me? Are you sure he was asking for me? I can't believe it. Are you quite sure? I mean . . .' Adah was becoming incoherent in her excitement. Her voice was loud and panicky.

'Yes, of course, dear, he came for you. Aahr, dear, don't cry,

8

it's going to be all right now. He's coming soon,' Mrs Devlin assured her.

Adah did not realise that her eyes were watering. She wiped her face, peered at the thin face of Mrs Marshall to make sure she was not dreaming, and in response Mrs Marshall pulled her dog to herself, nodding intermittently. 'It is true, it is true.'

Yes, it must be true, but she still had to fetch her babies from the nursery. The day was too good to be ruined by Matron's anger. The matron of her kids' nursery had become a friend, but was very keen on punctuality. She never hid the fact that she too had children of her own who would be waiting for her at home. So mothers were usually begged to come for their babies on time. Though she was so happy about Mrs Devlin's announcement, though she was dying to see the manager himself and get all the particulars, she would rather have taken the risk of missing all these than face an angry matron. She had a frightening anger, that matron had.

Aloud she said, 'I must get the children first, otherwise I'll get told off by the matron.'

'That's all right, you run along and get them; we'll wait for him when he comes. I am so happy for yer.'

She thanked Mrs Devlin and ran excitedly to the nursery. She picked up the baby from the pram where she had been left in the clean hospital-like room. The babies' room was painted blue with blue and pink teddies painted all over the blue furniture. Even the drinking mugs had teddies drawn on them. Did babies, when only four months old, really take notice of all those teddies, or were the teddies for the delight of the plump nurses with merry faces and fixed smiles? Her baby was gurgling at nothing in the pram. She even gave a smile of recognition when she saw her mother. Adah did not have much time to talk to her as she was supposed to be doing. It took her a long time to learn this ritual of talking to a baby who either did not understand or in most cases did not know what to make of it. In England they said it was very good to chatter to your child, even when it was a few hours old, so she too started doing it, but would make sure that none of her people were around. They might well think her a witch, talking to something that did not answer back.

In the toddlers' room there was always noise and clatter. Shrill repetitive and nerve-racking voices piped in the air. The nurses clad in their shapeless flowered overalls moved about in the confusion, soothing, separating, yelling and laughing alternately. The floor was cluttered with children's litter. Toys of all shapes – kangaroos, lizards, ducks – all sorts. Some were very good, soft and cuddly, though in most cases the little devils would rather throw them at one another than play with them.

One of the nurses, on seeing Adah, made several attempts to call her children away from the confusion, but the kids found it funny to pretend not to hear her. Adah, annoyed, marched into the confusion, pulled Bubu, one of her two boys, by the collar, but he jerked away and she had to let him go for fear of dropping the baby. Triumphant, Bubu laughed and invited his mother to 'chase me, Mummy, you can't catch me, you can't catch me'. Luckily for Adah, a nurse saw her predicament and, marching in like a sergeant-major, took Bubu and his younger sister Dada by the hand to the cloakroom for their coats. The kids protested fiercely, 'I don't want to go home, I want to play.'

'You'll come back tomorrow, then if the weather is nice we'll go to the park, we'll go by bus, we'll . . .' The nurse went on and on, telling them what they were going to do 'tomorrow'. To kids tomorrow is always a long time away and they would scarcely remember what it was the nurse had said the day before. She went on cooing to them in that sugary tone some people reserve for kids. They eventually came out of the nursery.

The next argument was who was to be on the right or the left of the baby's pram. Bubu said he had been on the right of the pram in the morning, and would now stay on the left. Dada said she took the left first, and was not going to give it up. She looked determined, clutching the coveted side with her little

10

hands, and leaning her head against it. Bubu tried to pull her away, and Adah commanded him to stop. 'Tomorrow you'll be on the left.' Bubu was pacified, especially as Adah agreed with him that Dada was a naughty girl and would not have sweets tomorrow.

She hurried them home as fast as she could in the circumstances. Coming into her street, she could see that the man was already waiting for her. She quickened her pace and the children on either side of her started to trot, just like horses, their unworn gloves dangling lifelessly from the sleeves of their coats.

The man who was waiting for her was in his mid-thirties, with his belly slightly protruding. With a belly like that he must watch his diet, his beer . . . 'Hello,' she said breathless.

The man seemed unsure of what he should do next. He had glasses, his grey top coat was unbuttoned, revealing a very clean shirt. The glasses he had on gave him a highly intelligent look, but he ruined the effect by keeping his mouth open most of the time. With his mouth opened like that he looked both intelligent and stupid simultaneously.

He decided to come to the point. 'Are you Mrs Obi?'

'Of course.'

She wondered why professionals ask this sort of question. What exactly was she supposed to do, wear a label? Of course she was Mrs Obi. She was beginning to hate the suspense. 'Have you a flat for me?' She might as well know the worst. This man now managed to look like both a sharp plain-clothes detective and a mere clerk.'

He cleared his throat. There was nothing to clear – he was just embarrassed or something. 'Yes, we've got temporary accommodation for you at the Pussy Mansions, not very far, just around the corner.'

'Come now, that's unfair,' Mrs Devlin cried. 'Why do you put a girl like her in such a Godforsaken place? Her children are very young, and she's very hard working. It's not fair at all. Why, she might as well stay where she is now!'

'Huh?' cried Adah wondering whether Mrs Devlin had gone mad. 'Stay here? You must be joking. Any hole is better than this filth.'

This pleased the man in the grey coat, and he gave Mrs Devlin a why-don't-you-shut-your-mouth sort of look. Mrs Devlin went on protesting.

'It's a rough place to put a girl like that.'

The grey-coated man felt that he had to volunteer an explanation as Adah was beginning to look at him dubiously. 'You see, we have to rehouse you rather quickly because we were told about the kind of bitter experiences you are being subjected to and gather that this place is not very safe for your children. You are going to stay at the Mansions for a short while – just a temporary arrangement, nothing permanent at all. Of course you can reject the offer if you don't particularly like it.'

He started to dangle two keys in front of Adah's face as if tantalising her. 'Take it or leave it!' his attitude seemed to be saying.

His cuff links were real gold, and his wrist-watch was golden too. He probably was the manager after all. The keys kept on dangling in front of her. Should she refuse the offer to save Mrs Devlin the humiliation of being slighted? Should she accept the offer just to move away from the oppressive situation she was in? *Poor Mrs Devlin, you don't know the gripping fears I go through every time I leave my children indoors to do some shopping, you don't know what it is like to realise that all your letters are being opened and read before you lay your hands on them, and you cannot dream what independence it is to have your own front door, your own toilet and bath, just for you and your family.*

Her feelings were transparent, and Mrs Devlin started to shuffle her way inside. Adah took the keys from the man very quickly. The man's mouth opened wider, surprised. He collected himself with a jerk, and said, 'You'll let us know tomorrow if you are going to accept it, won't you, so that the flat could be redecorated for you?'

It had taken Adah nine months of court-going, letter-writing and tribunal-visiting to get her this much. Now this man wanted her to approve first of all, then wait for redecoration before moving in; he must be out of his mind.

'I'm moving in tonight!'

'What?' The man jumped to attention as if giving a military salute. 'Are you quite sure madam? We don't want to rush you, and we always want our tenants to move into clean flats, you know, we could have it done over for you.'

'Is there any law preventing me from moving in today? Is there any law preventing you and your people from decorating when we've already moved in?'

'Of course not, madam.' The man began to look over his shoulder as if he was about to sell Adah some stolen goods. 'In that case, er, I do wish you a happy stay at the Mansions. Er . . . if you want anything, we will do the best we can. Goodbye.'

He turned around, walked quickly round the corner and disappeared, leaving Adah with the keys, and a hollow in her stomach, as if she had not eaten for days. She was going to take the flat and move out of this horrible place. She couldn't care less if in doing so she was offending a friend like Mrs Devlin – it was her own life. Why couldn't people leave her to make her own mistakes? She was going to take the flat. She must move, and move that very night.

Having collected her two older youngsters from school, Adah avoided Mrs Devlin for the rest of the evening. She did not wish to sing her joy aloud in case the landlord and landlady should guess that she was up to something. With suppressed excitement she told her children, the ones who were old enough to understand. 'We can't believe it,' they had chorused. She sped to the newsagent round the corner, and the man agreed to move her few possessions to the Mansions for her for thirty shillings. It was then the thought occurred to her that she had not even seen the flat. She sped down the road to the block. So this was the block of flats.

The outside looked like a prison, red bricks with tiny yellow windows. The shape of the whole block was square, with those tiny windows peeping into the streets. The block looked dependable, solid. The outside look was not too encouraging, but she must not despair. She went round in circles looking for an opening into the block, found one eventually, but it was so dark that she was not at first sure that she was not walking into a cave. She emerged into an open space, with a crowd of children playing.

She looked on both sides of her, feeling lost. She saw a little boy with a friendly face and asked him where flat number X was.

The boy looked at her and said, 'They moved yesterday, they've moved to Hampstead.'

Adah thanked him, and told him that she was going to be the new tenant, and asked him could he please show her where the flat was. The body did not look too happy at this question. He seemed to consider it for a while, shrugged his little shoulders as if to say, 'After all, what must be, must be.' He got up reluctantly and took her up what seemed to Adah to be ten flights of stone steps. She had never climbed such steep steps in her life, and at that speed too.

When they got to the top, the boy pointed to a door by a gaping chute. 'There it is.' He waited for Adah to open the door. She did, and the boy peeped inside just once and ran away, his mind already preoccupied with something else.

Adah went in, gingerly at first, inspecting one room after the other. It was not bad at all compared to what she had. She was very pleased with the bath in particular. All these rooms, just for her – well, God was wonderful. He had heard her prayers. Oh, yes, they were going to spend the night there. She went down the stairs quickly, ran down to her old house, calling on the newsagent on her way, picked up her odds and ends, and two hours later she was a tenant of the Mansions.

On that first night they had no beds, no curtains and no floor coverings, but Adah made do with an oil heater and piles of old

14

blankets and bed sheets. There were three important things she knew she had acquired that night, her independence, her freedom, and peace of mind.

3 *Pussy Cat Mansions*

The Pussy Cat Mansions were built round a large compound. Adah called the open space a compound, remembering Africa. The Family Adviser, whom she met later, used the word courtyard for the open space. It was an open space into which all the front doors opened out. In the centre of the compound were some ill-looking buildings. Adah's African friends called these little houses 'Juju man's house'. When the vicar's wife visited, she said to Adah, 'Those houses look like a monastery,' but the Deaconess said they looked more like a mortuary. Originally the architect had meant them to be used as pram and bicycle sheds, but by the time Adah moved into the Mansions the sheds had deteriorated so much that few mums would dream of putting their prams in them.

The Mansions' kids decided to make better use of these ill-looking buildings. They would rescue any piece of old furniture, any piece of old clothing, or any type of article which they fancied from the rubbish dumps, and deposit them in the little houses. The little houses ended up by looking more like a hippy shrine than anything else.

There were nearly one hundred and forty flats in the Mansions. The ground-floor flats were mainly one-room flats for the very old and infirm. The arrangement was perfect as most of the old people at the Mansions had meals brought to them 'on wheels', and the people who brought the meals were saved from climbing those endless stairs. The only disadvantage was the Mansions' children. The open space was used by them as a playground and on summer evenings looked like a circus. Big boys and girls cycled round the little houses, dogs barking and yelping at their heels; some boys played organised games of football, while many more would engage in just throwing balls, broken milk bottles and stones at random. Of course the old folk on the ground floor were usually the victims of the noise, the stone-throwing and the dogs' barking. There was little they could do about it so they just accepted things as they were.

Probably the old folk consoled themselves with the fact that, after all, they did not have long to live. To save them from unnecessary accidents, most of their windows had barbed wire fixed on them, just like prison windows of murderers awaiting execution. The barbed wire was meant to protect the glass from the boys' balls smashing it, but the picture it gave was that of condemnation, unwantedness and death – so impersonal and unclean did it look.

The stairs leading to the top flats were of grey stone, so steep were they that it took Adah and her kids weeks to get used to them. They were always smelly with a thick lavatorial stink. Most of the rubbish chutes along the steps and balconies were always overflowing and always open, their contents adding to the stink. The walls along the steep steps were of those shiny, impersonal bricks still seen in old tube stations, but even more like those Adah had seen in films of prisons. The windows were small and so were the doors. Most of the flats were dark in sympathy with the dark atmosphere. Ah, yes, the Mansions were a unique place, a separate place individualised for 'problem families' Problem families with real problems were placed in a problem place. So even if one lived at the Mansions and had no problems the set-up would create problems – in plenty.

Adah's problems were many. How to study, keep her job and look after the kids. Looking after her children was one of the problems created for her by the Mansions' set-up. In her old place her fear was that the landlord might harm them. At the Mansions, it was a different fear: offending the neighbours.

The walls separating one flat from the other were so thin that you could hear your next-door neighbour cough. In such a set-up how could a single girl keep four active children and a yelling baby from disturbing the neighbours?

Three days after she moved into the Mansions a man, a very angry man but very small indeed, knocked at her door. She was so surprised at the loudness of the knock that she went to the door with a frown on her face. She staggered backwards at the small man's voice, which was so big that she was tempted to look behind him for another owner of the voice. It was so incredible, such a loud voice from such a small man. Somebody said somewhere that Mother Nature is always logical. Well, with this Mr Small, she had miscalculated.

'Look!' he thundered, not bothering to introduce himself or excuse himself. 'Look, I don't mind your colour!'

Adah jumped. Colour, what colour was he talking about; she had never seen Mr Small before; what colour was he referring to? Well, human nature being what it is, Adah looked at the colour of the back of her hand; well, yes. Mr Small did not mind the colour brown, now what next? What was the next thing he did not mind about? Mr Small's eyes followed her movements and smiled. Happy. He had put Adah in her place. A black person must always have a place, a white person already had one by birthright.

'My baby is only three weeks old,' he went on. 'You and your kids kept him awake all night. What did you think you were doing, eh? And you walking about with them army boots. I won't have it, I am warning yer.'

Adah was puzzled. She tried to work out the argument in her mind. But two points did not quite fit in. One was her colour, which Mr Small did not mind, and secondly the army boots. So she asked, 'Are you sure you heard army boots in the night? You see, there is no man here and I don't wear army boots, because, you see, I've never been in the army.'

18

Mr Small went hysterical and his equally little wife joined him. It seemed that since Adah and her kids moved into the Mansions the Small family had never had a moment's peace. This brought out Mr Small's mother, a little woman with white hair and white whiskers. Adah knew that to argue was going to be a losing battle. She was made to understand by Granny Small that Mr Small had been born in the Mansions and that Mrs Small had also been born in the Mansions, in the flat just opposite. Adah got the message, she was dealing with The Establishment, one of the original clans of the Mansions who had lived there for thirty years. She was being told to mind her ways, because the Council would rather listen to reports from the Mansions' senior citizens than to the story of a newcomer. It was going to be a case of her story against theirs.

'I am sorry about the disturbance. I'll tell the kids to make less noise.' That was her first mistake. At the Mansions, it was not normal to apologise. Even when you were caught stealing, you had to argue your way out. If arguments failed, you could always fight your way out of any mess. To say you were sorry was like signing your death warrant. It was a sign of weakness. You were inviting the other person to overcome you, suppress you.

The Smalls seemed happy to show Adah their new baby. So Adah's old man had deserted her? They tut-tutted their sympathy. Of course she could always ask them for any help. They were always willing to help.

The Smalls were just one of the few families in the Mansions who started poor and ended up rich – rich by Mansions' standards, at any rate. There was the Granny Small who had come to the Mansions as a widow thirty years before with six children. Most of them had married and gone, leaving Mr Small and his pretty wife. Mr Small worked as a plumber for the Council, and tradition had it that he was very hard-working and that the family were consequently very rich. They got everything from the Mothercare shop, and they wanted the dregs – the usual unmarried mothers, or the wife of 'Bill who was sent down the other day' – to know that they were in a class higher.

Adah knew that to quarrel with their type would be useless, so she decided to be friends. But how did one become friends with someone who believed himself to be superior, richer and made of a better clay? Still, she was determined to try.

One of the methods she had found very helpful in securing friendship in England was to pretend to be ignorant. You see, if you were black and ignorant, you were conforming to what society expected of you. She was determined to try it with the Smalls.

Her opportunity came the next day. It had been very wet, and she was beginning to realise how damp it could be in the Mansions' flats. Some men were delivering coalite and, seeing the Smalls buying some, she thought she might buy some too. She thought coalite would be easy to light. She tried and tried again, but the coalite did not start. She knew she could pour paraffin on it and start it quickly, but was not quite sure that would not start an uncontrollable fire.

With her eyes streaming from smoke, and her hands blackened by the coalite, she came out of the balcony and luckily Granny Small was standing there.

'Please, how do I light the coalite? I don't seem to be getting it right.' Granny Small turned and faced her. Her eyes were bloodshot. Adah regretted her impulsive gesture immediately. She should have stayed indoors, she should have kept trying until she got it right. She could not go back now without appearing eccentric. So she repeated her plea, now in a voice unnecessarily loud.

'I can't light my coalite.'

'Well, why did you buy it? What am I supposed to do about it, eh?'

The pretty wife shot out. 'What was it, Mum?'

'She couldn't light the coalite.' Well, what were they going to hear next?

Adah pointed out that she knew she could start it with paraffin, but would it start a fire?

The pretty wife screamed. 'Mum, she's going to bring in the firemen soon. Oh, my God, what are we in for!' Her shrieking voice brought out more neighbours, some to see what the matter was, but most to have a good look at the new tenant as if she was a wonder from outer space.

This method had never failed her before. Why did it fail with the Smalls? They did not even give her time to get to know her before they passed their judgement. Being friendly with them would be out of the question. She would have to mind her own business. What these people felt towards her was resentment. She had worsened the situation by letting them know that she had never used coalite before. How could she have known how to use coalite? She had been born and brought up in the tropics where the average daily temperature was in the eighties. How could people be so ignorant? The funniest thing was that from the cynical remarks being made around her, it was implied that she must be illiterate not to know how to use coalite.

What was the point in explaining to them that in her country she attended a colonial school with a standard equalling the best girls' school in London? What was the point in telling them that she was not illiterate as they thought, and that even here in their country she worked in their Civil Service. She looked at them, felt a little bit like being sick, then walked in, shutting her front door behind her with a loud bang.

Inside she poured paraffin on some paper, and started the fire. She did not have to call in the firemen, because there was no need for them. She did not burn the flats down.

Adah knew that her problems were going to be many, for the Smalls seemed determined to add to the fact that she would have to worry about keeping her job, worry about how to study, and now worry how to keep the kids quiet. If the Mansions' tenants did not want her, well, she was going to be different. She was not going to be like the other separated mums. At the Mansions, women with kids and no husbands did not go out to

21

work. It was just not done. If you were separated, you lived on the dole. 'I am going to be different,' Adah said to herself in consolation, little realising that she more than anybody else would need people to talk to and be friendly with. For she was human, and a lonely woman.

She not only had to conform but, for peace's sake, she had to belong. She had to belong, socialise, participate in the goings-on.

4 *Baptism by Socialisation*

'Mummy, what are we having for tea tonight? I'm so hungry now,' Bubu said, coming to the kitchen door.

'We are going to have baked beans and chips; I am going to make them very nice. Will you eat a lot?'

'Oh, yeah, yummy!' Bubu replied, rubbing his palms on his little tummy. Adah laughed and promised that she was not going to take very long.

'What are you rubbing your tummy like that for?' Titi, the eldest girl, asked from the doorway, where she was sitting and playing with a naked doll. 'It's childish to rub your tummy like that.'

'Well, it's my tummy, aren't it, Mummy?' Bubu wanted to know. Adah agreed with him that the tummy was his and that he was free to do whatever he liked with it.

The arguments that would have followed were prevented by a tap on their front door.

Adah quickly snatched the opportunity and said, 'Open the door, Titi, and see who is there,' as she craned her neck from the kitchen into the doorway to see who it was.

'Mum, it's a lady, she wants to see yer, Mum,' Titi announced rather shrilly.

'Can't these Jehovah's Witnesses leave you alone? They visit you at awkward times, and expect you to leave all and follow them to save you from Armageddon which they claim is perpetually round the corner,' Adah was growling to herself when Titi repeated her announcement. This made Adah throw off her colourful wrapper, which she tied on her work dress, to prevent oil from soiling it. There was not time to wash her hands because the 'lady' was in the hallway already.

'Hello,' cooed the lady. Her voice was low and professional. She was large, fleshy and hippy, like a rich African mammy after a session in a fattening room. Her hair was blondish, thin and short. She had rows and rows of brown beads around her thick neck. The neck was short with folds of flesh. Everything about the lady was big, except her feet. The feet were surprisingly small. Her files, her bag, were all large. She purred her second hello. The look she gave Adah was deep, searching and suspicious.

Adah helloed back. Her hello was distant, uncertain and rather faint. She was not quite sure whether to shake hands or give a bow of the head, or do both. Instead she smiled wanly and tried not to appear too eager to please.

'I don't think we've met before. I work here, and my name is Carol. I am the Family Adviser. Are these your children?'

She's come to tell me something nasty and she's nervous, Adah thought. The lady started to ramble on about the flats, the weather, and any other blatant nothings her large mind could think of. Getting neither response nor encouragement from Adah, the large lady decided to come to the point.

'People here,' she spread her fat short arms, 'say that your children make too much noise, and that you leave them all by themselves in the evenings.'

These nosey parkers all pretend to mind their own business, but they don't, Adah thought. 'So you come to take them away from me, lady?' she asked aloud.

'Oh, no. I only want you to check them.'

'But I do! I really do!' Adah cried. Her mouth tasted bitter. 'Do they look noisy and unchecked? Do they, now you tell me?'

'No, I'm afraid not,' replied the lady diplomatically. Her reply was too hasty to be sincere, and it sounded a bit hollow. 'But that's the report I have, so I thought I should let you know. Don't take it too seriously; we all have our problems, dear.'

Adah's mind was full. She was not interested in the lady's problems; if she had any real problems, she wouldn't be so bulky. She was worrying about her own problems. What was God's purpose in creating people like her? To be born just to keep tasting bitterness and sorrow and simply watch other humans getting all the goodies. All she had ever known in all her life was sorrow, anxiety and endless bitterness. These neighbours, the ones that the lady was talking about, must be the Smalls. They had so successfully conditioned her that she could hardly listen to the news on her radio without a pang of guilt. She had stopped doing her own sewing because the hum of the machine disturbed them. What exactly was she expected to do now? Stop caring? Give in to sorrow and stop trying?

'What are you going to do to us now, lady? Send me to jail or to my Maker?' She might as well be told the truth.

But the lady was a true diplomat, a trained and experienced social worker, one of a race of women whom one was never sure whether to treat as friends or as members of the social police. The lady had been reading her, of course.

'Don't call me "lady", I am Carol. Everybody calls me Carol. Please call me Carol,' said Carol lyrically. She heaved her large bust, ran her fingers through her rows of beads, and quickly changed the subject. 'I see you are a Ghanaian.'

'I am not a Ghanaian,' Adah snapped, wondering what her nationality had to do with it. People in Adah's position are usually on the defensive all the time. Even when shown kindness or politeness, they usually don't know what to do with it. Instead they grow suspicious and remote.

Carol was waiting for an explanation. She'd heard that Adah did not come from Ghana, then where did she come from? she seemed to be wordlessly demanding. But Adah refused to talk. Carol sensed that Adah wanted her to go, but she did not want to leave just yet.

They simply stared at each other.

25

'The kids' food is getting cold,' remarked Carol rather abruptly.

'Yes, thank you, they must be very hungry by now. You must excuse me.'

Adah went back into the kitchen and reheated the beans. 'Supper!' she shouted.

The kids hurried into the kitchen and Adah dished out the food. The usual talk and arguments started.

'Stop kicking me, you monster! I'm telling Mummy of you, stare cat!'

'Isn't it lovely,' Carol observed, bending her thick neck to one side. In another woman the attitude and posture she adopted would have been feminine and maternal, but her bulk robbed her of all those qualities. No wonder they made her the Family Adviser. Her weight would crush any family problems, however thorny, into powder. She was trying very hard to make Adah realise that she loved kids.

Adah knew that it was a put-on show, but for that moment at least she was mollified, in fact flattered that anyone else could love her little terrors. Her anger of a minute ago gone, she volunteered: 'I am an Igbo, from Lagos. My parents came here from Igbo land, but I was born and grew up in Lagos and from there I came to London.'

'I see,' drawled Carol. Her smile was wide and full of understanding. Her face betrayed a happy relief. 'I stayed six years in Africa myself, mostly in Aden, but I paid a short visit to West Africa, stayed a year in Ghana, and six months in Lagos. It's a lovely place. Beautiful.'

Everybody seemed to know Lagos. The charwoman in her office had a son who lived at Apapa in Lagos; the man from the Coal Board who came the day before to inspect her fireplace knew all about Lagos. The trouble was you couldn't even lie about your home anymore. Before you opened your mouth, your listener knew all about what you were going to say. It made life so dull. Even the people in some part of the world who for generations had happily worshipped the moon because

26

it was a mystery had now had their mystery unveiled. Adah was sure that those in Society beginning with a capital S would soon be going to the moon either to holiday or to play golf, or for some training in the kangaroo walk. *Well, lady, if you know about Lagos, congratulations.*

'Please call on me at any time. The little house by the side of the playground is my office. Kids are free to play there. I have educational toys and mums do meet occasionally in my office. I know you are very busy, but do come down sometimes.' She made as if to go, but halfway down the hallway, she asked all of a sudden, 'Where do you go in the evenings?'

Adah had sensed that the lady was holding something back. She would make a good sales woman. She might be social police, but at least she was being nice about policing. She did not feel like lying to the lady, so she told her that she was a sociology student, and that she attended classes in the evenings.

Carol padded back. Her shoes were flat, almost like bedroom slippers. That was sensible, otherwise her walk would be an unpleasant wobble.

'Who looks after the children when you go?' Her voice had become professional again, with a tinge of harshness in it, like that of a woman who had spent all her life doing things for other people.

'They look after themselves,' explained Adah, sounding like a condemned criminal. She did not only sound like one, she was beginning to feel like one.

'You're not allowed to do that. Not in London.' Carol shook her head from side to side. 'You could be in trouble for that, real trouble. Things are different here. I know that in Africa neighbours are free to come and go, because your doors are always open to let in cool air, but in England we shut our doors to keep out cold air. So people can't tell when kids who are by themselves get into trouble. Anything could happen – a gas explosion, oil heaters starting big fires, oh, all sorts of things. You do understand, I am sure.'

27

Adah understood all right, but what was she to do? She did not like the idea of packing up her studies, since she'd got that far, and yet did not want anything to happen to her kids. She looked sadly at nothing. Her mind was so muddled she could think of nothing.

Carol sensed that she was dealing with a woman who would give everything for her children. She was right. Adah's children were her life. Anyone who loved them loved her.

'I'll see that you get some help, in the evenings at least. You're doing too much, biting off more than you can chew.'

That was one of the things Adah did not like about these white-coated females who called themselves social officers. They were bloody well too patronising. All right, she had pointed out that Adah was wrong in leaving her kids in the evenings – why make a meal of it? Well, the lady seemed to care, even if society had to pay her to care. Adah would have to swallow her pride as a woman, her dignity as a mother, and let Carol help her. She did not like to accept the help, but she had no choice. She needed to be protected against troublesome neighbours like the Smalls and she wanted the assurance of knowing that her children were in good hands when she was at the Polytechnic. She was grateful to the lady, and had to thank her.

She saw the lady to the door, and was not at all surprised to see the fast-disappearing figures of the Smalls as they rushed back into their flat. They had been listening. They had sent Carol, but Adah was determined to make the best use of Carol's services.

Adah did not need to make too much effort to be friends with Carol. The Family Adviser took a real liking to her. She got in contact with Task Force and they sent a group of young students who had volunteered to look after Adah's children in the evenings. Adah was not sure how to behave to these young people with their unisex fashions. It was actually impossible to tell who was male and who was female; they all looked alike.

Nevertheless Adah welcomed them and hoped they would be at home in her flat.

The first evening when the 'sitters' came she kept worrying in the class at the Poly. She held herself to her seat from sheer will power. Society had nothing good to say about long-haired, guitar-playing Youth. All she had read and heard about them was that they were always marching from pillar to post with their mad banners, they were always sitting-in somewhere or other, and almost all of them were on dope. Suppose they should start smoking the stuff in the presence of her kids? Suppose they started their free love while the kids were still awake? Oh, God, help her. As soon as it was nine o'clock she sped home.

She could not help crying quietly to herself at what she saw. Her children had been washed, her bathroom was spring-cleaned, and the sitting-room was swept. Yes, the young people sat and watched television, holding hands in such a gentle resigned way that Adah's heart went out to them. She put on a bold face. 'After all, I am older than they are, almost ten years older, why should I be so unsure in their presence, and in my own house too! Blast it all, I should put them in their place, not they me,' she told herself. Aloud, she scolded them for not taking the tea she told them to. They should feel at home, she went on babbling, while the youths giggled in their tired limpid way. She fed them on seasoned rice and lemon tea, and they said that it was nice. But she was sure that the tears flowing from their eyes were not from joy but because the curried rice was too peppery. They drank gallons of water and went back to the college.

The young man's name was Jerry, but Adah did not catch the name of the girl, not that it was even necessary for her to know it, because Jerry took delight in changing his girlfriends as other less well-endowed males do their shirts. These young people almost became members of Adah's family. They would wash nappies, feed the children and would even go out of their way to come and take the children out at weekends. Till her

29

dying day, Adah would still wonder why overstuffed middle-aged individuals painted all young people as irresponsible, rootless and shiftless. No one ever publicised the good works they did. No one ever hinted that many of them joined organisations like Task Force. No one ever thought it worth-while to say anything about their sympathy and understand-ing. Some of the youths might go to extremes, but hadn't the older generations got their eccentricities too?

Adah came to look forward to their coming, and through Jerry she came to know not just a lot of English girls but also some exotic French and Italian girls who came to England to study.

The Family Adviser paid her another visit, and Adah wondered what it was she had done wrong. She put on an unhappy face waiting for the bombshell. As usual Carol started with her banalities.

'This is fufu?' she said commenting on the children's food.

'No, not really, we can't get fufu here so we make do with ground rice,' Adah explained in reply.

'It's a cheap sort of food, don't you think?' Carol wanted to know.

'Well, I don't think I know anything about it's being cheap, but I do know that it's filling.'

'Hm,' murmured Carol nodding her head, and the folds of fat around her neck danced. 'Do the children like it? Don't they think it's hot?'

'Do English children like potatoes, don't they think they're tasteless?'

'I am being stupid,' Carol conceded.

'Perhaps so.' Adah was in no mood to be humble, and wished to God Carol would have her say and leave her alone.

'The schoolmistress complained to me that the children are being left in the school sheds at eight in the mornings and that you don't come for them until five o'clock. She can't be responsible for them before school starts, you know. The mornings are too cold and dark to leave them alone. You know, don't you, that some sick people snatch children, and yours are so young, anyone could tempt them away with ordinary sweets.'

Adah's tears started to flow. Those horrible tears, always flowing at the wrong moment. She wanted to appear bold, to tell Carol to mind her own business, but could not. She was worried about the children, too, so worried that it told on her job. Though she was lucky to be working with very understanding people, she knew that bosses could not go on being accommodating for ever. She had taken all her holidays, maternity leave, compassionate leave and every other sort of leave the Civil Service could think of allowing people like her. There was a limit to human sympathy, even that of the bosses.

She wiped away her tears. Immediately, her mind made up, she threw her decision at Carol.

'I am resigning my job at the Museum!'

'Oh, dear, that's a hasty decision to make. I'm sorry if I am responsible for the rush. We'll think up another way. . . .'

Adah cut her short with determination. 'There is no other way, and please for God's sake stop blaming yourself. I've thought about it for a long time.'

Her socialisation was complete. She, an African woman with five children and no husband, no job, and no future, was just like most of her neighbours – shiftless, rootless, with no rightful claim to anything. Just cut off . . . none of them knew the beginning of their existence, the reason for their hand-to-mouth existence, or the result or future of that existence. All would stay in the ditch until somebody pulled them out or they sank under.

The Museum was happy to get rid of her though too polite to say so. That closed her middle-class chapter. From then on, she belonged to no class at all. She couldn't claim to be working-class, because the working class had a code for daily living. She had none. Hers was then a complete problem family. Joblessness baptised her into the Mansions' society. Like most of the tenants there, she became a regular visitor at Carol's office.

31

She was introduced to Whoopey and her mother. Mrs O'Brien and the Princess smiled their welcome into the ditch-dwellers' cult. She joined the ditch-dwellers' association. She joined the mothers' local socials. She resigned herself to the mysterious inevitability and accepted things as they were.

The smiles and limpid nods of these faded and rejected women reassured her. They seemed to say, 'You are not alone. Look at us, we are humans too!' She was comforted by the warmth of their acceptance, and was thankful.

5   *Down to the Dole House*

'You must go on the dole,' the Family Adviser advised, weeks after Adah had left work. 'You have to live somehow; you must try for the dole. Everybody does when in need. You are even lucky, because you'll only be on Assistance for a time. What about women who will never be able to earn enough to keep themselves? I should go if I were you, for the children's sake.'

'Yes, for the children's sake,' Adah's voice was faint and distant. But had she any choice? To refuse Assistance would have been empty pride – pride which originated from the fact that in her country she had learned that the Ministry of Social Security was the modern version of the old Poor Law. She had come to think of those on the dole as lazy, parasitic people who lived off Society. She had dreamt that she would be writing African short stories, but her attempts in the past weeks had resulted in nothing but the constant appearance of rejection slips. She had had so many of these nicely worded rejection documents that her dream of being an author had vaporised. She had plunged her hands into the sixty pounds she had saved from her Museum job.

Hot peppery tears almost blinded her eyes one morning when she stared at her savings book to find she had only fifty shillings left. She did not wait for Carol to preach her duty to her any more. She must live somehow. Going on the dole was better than stealing. She picked up two of her smallest children and they all trooped to the Dole House.

33

You never knew, Carol might be right. 'I may not have to be on the dole for long,' she thought. 'I may still become a writer, a writer of a best-selling book, I may still become a qualified social scientist who may one day be an adviser like Carol. Meanwhile, I must live, and I must look after the kids that God gave me alive. God made a little mistake there though. He should have allowed each child that arrived a sack of money, instead of the sack of useless after-birth.'

She pulled herself together and faced reality . . . the board in front of the building read 'The Department of . . .' what and what else. Adah did not bother to read it to the last letter. Funny calling the Dole House social security. Whatever security the sign board might promise her, she began to feel insecure as soon as she stepped into the building, wheeling her two kids.

The Dole House was painted yellow, an impersonal sort of blank yellow. There was a wire screen in the centre which divided the oblong into two rectangles. The inner rectangle was for the staff, the outer one for people like Adah, those who came to be doled to. Benches were placed for people to sit on. The faces of those on the benches showed dejection, boredom, hopelessness and self-pity. Adah sat on one of the benches facing the inquiry desk.

Her turn came after what seemed ages of bottom-shifting and feet-shuffling. You shifted and shuffled to the next empty space on the bench until finally you came face to face with the person behind the screen. The person wanted to know the history of your existence, whether you'd been inside, and if so, whether it was Brixton or Holloway. In the end, your life and secrets were reduced to a 'yes' and 'no' table.

The female was genuinely interested in Adah's case, though. Resigning from the Civil Service at twenty-five! 'You'll lose your pension,' the clerk cried. 'Don't you know what that means? You should have stayed.'

Adah was full of excuses. She repeated her explanation of why she had to give up her work. Yes, she *was* happy at the job,

34

but she had had to leave all the same. The clerk reluctantly agreed that her reasons were, after all, sensible.

'Take your seat over there, you'll be called soon.'

Adah found a vacant space on one of the benches and sat down. After all, she had told the clerk everything there was to tell, and she would be called soon.

She forgot that the word 'soon' can be days, hours or even years. She had thought that 'soon' in this particular context would be at most thirty minutes or so.

Her children started to fidget and whine after two hours' waiting.

'Mum, I want to go the toilet – oh, please, it's coming down, Mum – *please!*'

Desperate, Adah dashed to a man in uniform, who looked like the caretaker. 'Please could you tell me where the toilet is? My little girl is very pressed.'

The man looked vacantly at her, as is she were a half-witted woman who had long taken leave of her senses. He smiled indulgently and pointed to the notice at one side of the wall which said that the toilet was somewhere up the road.

'Mum, I'm doing it here,' shouted Dada, holding her pants tightly as if that would stop her pressing demands.

'Please, could she not use the staff toilet? She's only a little girl, please,' Adah begged, her voice unsteady.

'Sorry, they can't use our toilet. There is a public one near the Polytechnic. You know where it is?'

Adah knew.

Outside the fog was thick. The children and she joined it. Happy family! For breakfast the children had had a bowl of custard and a quarter of an orange each. They had left the Mansions at ten o'clock in the morning. It was already twelve-thirty, foggy, cold and November. It was human to wish to live as long as possible: even though sometimes life might be worthless, one still clung to it. That human wish to live, to survive, pushed her to the toilet. They relieved themselves, and trod their way back to the Dole House.

35

She took her seat by a woman with one large foot and one skinny one. She had a black shoe on the skinny one, but on the large one was a bit of sewn-up leather, with a mock heel underneath. She stared at Adah, a sign that she wanted to talk to her.

Adah smiled and the lady with the unequal feet said, 'Are you Mrs Obi? They were calling for you after you left.'

'Were they calling me for the money, do you know?' Her voice was loud and panicky, despite her put-on calm. A few well-dressed men sitting on the bench next to hers heard her and laughed. She looked round wildly. Had she said something outlandish?

'Not for the money, mate,' said a handsome man from the group. 'For inquiries,' he sneered, jerking his head insultingly in the direction of the officers behind the screened counter. This group of men were relaxed and looked carefree. They were strikers. 'You'll have to wait two more hours for that,' he said.

He was right. The woman with the large foot became friendly. 'I used to mind one of your people's children, you know. That was before I started having trouble with my foot. They were ever so nice, those people. The mother was just like you, you know, young and good clothes . . . very nice.'

Adah nodded, and wondered whether she was overdressed for the Dole House. She had come in a new trouser suit she had made from a pattern in a woman's magazine. It had cost her less than two pounds. Perhaps she was overdressed. Next time she must remember to come in old clothes, Mansions-style.

'Are you from Nigeria?' asked the woman.

'Yes,' she replied simply, not wanting to go into the details of why part of Nigeria had become Biafra and then gone back again to being part of Nigeria.

The woman was very lonely, for she talked and talked, with controlled gesticulation. Adah listened, fascinated. The woman had been to a Nigerian christening in London; she had also been to a Nigerian wedding at St Martin-in-the-Fields.

The first time she'd been to 'them poshy places'. Those were the days before 'me foot'.

Adah could well understand her curiosity. Her fellow countrymen and women in London *would* have their weddings in a 'poshy' place like St Martin-in-the-Fields. She knew of Arican couples who had insisted on a real red carpet for their weddings. It all sounded so funny – coming from a country where kids still died from malnutrition, where three-quarters of the population had never tasted clean tap water, where there were still all sorts of horrors arising from illiteracy, yet where they, the few so-called enlightened ones, blew what little money they had on such extravagances. Still, not to worry. Had not millions of pounds been spent on finding out more about the moon, while the problems on earth which were already known were swept under the carpet? It had gone out of fashion to say, 'I got married in a little church in England.' It would be equally boring to claim that, 'My country is doing all she can about the poor, the old and the needy, and because of this, she can't join the race to the moon.' British Africans tried very hard to show how affluent they were, even though the affluence rested uneasily, like borrowed robes. Learning to be a statesman was not an easy job.

It was just as funny to think that, but for the Nigerians, this woman whose parents and great-great-grandparents had always been white would never have been inside 'them poshy places'.

The wait at the Dole House was long, but the woman was happy for it. 'It saves me fires,' she confided. 'Do you like it here in England?'

'Immensely.' Adah was eager to please and guessed the woman wanted such an answer. She was shocked when the woman's reaction was different.

The woman laughed loudly. 'You've been here for some time, I can see that. You said that because you thought I'd like to hear you say it.'

Adah made a movement as if to protest, but the woman cut

her short and said, 'I know, I know, no Nigerian can tell *me* he or she is happy living here. You want your degree, or whatever it is, and then you'll be off home. Only Nigerian failures stay in England. You don't really like it here.'

Adah was silenced, not knowing what else to say.

'Funny, you're the first Nigerian I've heard say that. I can understand the West Indians saying it, but you . . . Oh, I don't know. . .'

The social security officers came to her rescue. Mrs Wilkinson was called for money. 'Ta ra, love,' she smiled, and bending down with obvious difficulty, she whispered, 'You hurry up and go home. You are not a failure, and you're not going to be.'

'Bye-bye,' Adah said, thankful to be alone at last.

Soon afterwards, she was called and given thirteen pounds – six pounds was to be for rent, a quid for gas, two for heating, and four for food.

There was a supermarket opposite the Social Security office, and as it was getting late, she thought she might as well do her shopping now. She got all the odds and ends she decided she would need and put them into the metal basket, but when she got to the cash assistant, she was surprised to learn that she had to pay five pounds. She had not intended to spend so much. Was it due to the dim light in the supermarket, or the lulling music after the harshness of the Dole House? Well, whatever it was, she just had to take the groceries, for she was too scared to return them. She would make it up from the allowance for heating. That would mean goodbye to coalite and a happy welcome to Blue Paraffin – after all, it said 'for the nobility' in the advertisements.

By the time she got home, the children were hungry and very tired. They had fallen asleep in the push-chair. She hurried, happy at the sight of food, cooked brown rice with chicken stew. One good meal a week at least, not bad, considering that she did not have to work for it.

Adah washed her face, put on an old dress, Mansions-style, and went down to Carol's place, which was quite near.

38

'Hi yer, Adah,' shouted Whoopey, a regular visitor at Carol's. 'You'd better come to the clothes exchange this evening.'

'Clothes exchange? I don't know, what is it?' Adah replied as she stepped in to the social workers' office.

'Well, it's really where you come for old clothes for children. We call it clothes exchange because mothers bring out-grown clothes from their homes and change them for something else,' Carol explained coolly, eyeing Adah calculatingly all the time. Her voice was a sharp contrast to Whoopey's high-pitched one.

'You pay a little contribution, though; not much, about a shilling or so, nothing much,' Carol finished.

'Now you know all about it,' said Mrs O'Brien, stuffing Carol's pieces of cake into the tiny mouth of her youngest baby. The baby tried to laugh with his mouth full, but ended by spitting crumbs of saliva-soaked cake on to Adah and Carol. They all laughed.

The office was warm, really warm. It was a three-roomed flat, converted into an office. Most of the windows had been broken by young hooligans who wanted to take – or at least to know – what Carol had in 'them soddin' cupboards'. On the walls were children's paintings of all descriptions, stuck up haphazardly as if by a blind person. Conversation buzzed, pots and pots of coffee went round. Carol talked and expanded. Plans which had little hope of fulfilment were put forward and for that particular moment everybody seemed taken in by them. None of the Mansions' mums sitting there and listening thought it out of place to make all these empty plans. Whoopey took up the thread of the empty dream and told them of the dream she had the night before.

'You know some'nk,' she started squeakily, 'you know some'nk, this handsome bloke, very dark, not black, you know. This bloke, 'e asked me to go on 'olidays with 'im and I did. When we were there, me kids, Sue and Terry, fell for 'im and called 'im dad. He loved them and loved me too. When we came home from the holidays the handsome bloke asked me to marry 'im, he did. He was ever so nice about it and me mum cried, she did. And you know some'nk, he was bloody rich, with pots and pots of money, and then he asked me and me kids to go to Australia with 'im and we did!' Whoopey ended breathlessly, her cigarette burnt low.

The silence that followed this dream recital was short, then Mrs Cox, Whoopey's mother, burst out, 'Yerse, and when you was in Australia, I'm sure you found out that he was a bleedin' train-robber – ha, ha, ha!'

'Oh, Mum, must you spoil it for me? I dreamt it last night, 'onest I did, Mum, I did,' Whoopey agonised.

'Yeah, you go and dream of how you're going to feed your bloody kids and clothe your skinny back. You're out of practice, mate, your arms are too fucking rusty for that sort of thing.'

At first Adah was shocked at this low language, but she came to know it meant nothing. The swearing adjectives were empty of meaning to the Mansions' women. Swearing meant nothing, it was just one of the ways of speaking at the Mansions.

It was Carol who started to laugh first, others were hesitant in joining. Carol confirmed that one never knew, such dreams might come true. One of her cases, an unmarried mother she knew somewhere, ended just like in Whoopey's dream.

'Yeah, and they lived happily ever after, I bet,' Mrs Cox concluded rather explosively.

'What time is it?' asked Mrs O'Brien.

'Three-thirty,' announced Carol.

The announcement made the chit-chat flag. Thoughts of kids at school needing to be brought home intervened.

Mrs O'Brien waddled towards the exit, strapped her baby to one of Carol's baby chairs and announced, 'Keep an eye on him for me,' to no one in particular.

Whoopey walked about with hip-swaying strides, collecting cups and saucers, and Adah coo-eed to Mrs O'Brien to wait for her. She must collect 'her two' from school.

Mrs Cox laughed loudly and rather mirthlessly at her

daughter. But Whoopey returned a gaze so cool and challenging that it made her mother shrink a bit. She stopped laughing, and the two watchful women by the exit walked out quickly.

6 *Happier on the Dole*

It was half-past three and Adah had to get her youngsters
from school. The weather had not been too good that summer.
Rain, rain, all the time. The rain would not have been taken so
badly at the Mansions if it had kept itself outside. But, oh, no,
not at the Mansions. Whenever it rained outside, it rained
inside.

Mildew carpeted most of the built-in cupboards. Ditch-
dwellers had long given up hope of scraping off the wretched
green stuff. What was the point of scraping the cupboards,
when to do so simply meant creating room for a fresh coat of
green? They let the mildew stay, so it became part of the
character of Mansions' cupboards. Adah greeted the mildew in
her scarf-cupboard with a soundless sigh. She took out her
favourite white scarf with the red border, shook it vigorously in
a vain attempt to get rid of the green smear, gave up the
attempt after many trials, and tied it securely under her chin.
She looked into a wall-mirror nearby and discovered that in her
attempt to cover the green smear she was showing the two holes
in the scarf. She unknotted it and tried again, putting the part
with the holes underneath, but the smear seemed to enjoy
showing itself to the world. She now had to choose whether to
show the mildew smear or the poverty holes. She decided in
favour of the smear – people might even think it was a pattern.
She shuffled her feet into an equally worn-out pair of shoes,
which must have seen far happier days before arriving at the

Mansions' clothes exchange. Good Lord, it was already twenty to four, she must fly!

She had to be careful over the wet slimy stairs (some teenagers had decided to make a toilet of them) especially as the light bulbs along the stairway had their own way of going out at night. Only God above could tell what usually happened to these temperamental bulbs. The caretaker swore that he had them replaced often enough, and would not appoint himself to watch over them. So if you were a ditch-dweller and did not want trouble, you had to plan your outings in the day when there was enough light.

Adah descended gingerly over the wet steps. The urinal smell mingled nicely with that from the gaping rubbish chutes. She had one short whiff of the smell when she was buttoning her coat and decided that that one was enough to last her till her feet were safely on the ground in the open compound. She covered her nose tightly, her eyes peeping from above her hand.

Mrs O'Brien too was coming from the other end, her hand over her nose and mouth, but Adah could see that her eyes lit up with happiness on seeing her. She too was going for some of 'hers' from school. They greeted each other mutely like dumb neighbours, and walked carefully down the stairs.

In the compound, they both took their hands off their faces, breathed in deep fresh air from the Mansions' compound, and smiled.

'I hate those filthy stairs,' remarked Mrs O'Brien unnecessarily.

'Me too,' Adah agreed, 'but I'm thankful the kids spend most of their time at school and do not have to run up and down them. They're so dangerous.'

Mrs O'Brien's face which had been alight with happiness a minute before crumpled in apparent distress. She shrugged her shoulders, clutched nervously at her shopping basket and furrowed her brows. She pulled the faded scarf which was slipping off her blondish hair into place, revealing fingernails that needed washing, hands that needed a good creaming.

'I don't know, love, I just don't know the right thing to do. I have two toddlers at home, you see, and they are always going up and down those dangerous stairs. Sometimes they even pick things up, well, you know what toddlers are, they like putting things into their mouths.'

'Oh, dear! That is serious. They can catch disease, they can.'

'That's what worries me, you see. I can't take them out with me all the time, and those social security officers would raise hell if they found out that I leave them to play by themselves. As you know, my old man's at home a lot, but you know what *men* are, they just don't *think*! Sometimes I take them to Carol's office, but as you know, she's not always there, and she's not always in the mood for kids.'

Adah nodded, as both women became preoccupied with the string of oncoming traffic. Soon the road was clear, and they dashed across it to the other side, into the Crescent (as Queen's Crescent was always called − no one locally allowed it its Christian name) Market.

They were met by a man selling some china and glassware. 'Beat the tax and buy now for Christmas!' he shrieked at them. Adah took a beautiful glass bird and admired it. Yes, the bird was beautiful and looked original. They assured the man that the price he was asking was very reasonable, and that was true. But the poor man wanted to sell his bird. He wanted them to buy. His voice was desperate and his mouth was dry as if he'd been shrieking for hours.

'It's lovely, love, but I have no money, not even a tanner to spare, love.' Mrs O'Brien sounded as if she was pleading with him.

He looked at Adah, his confidence slipping. 'You would like it, wouldn't you? I sold six to one of your people yesterday; the gentleman was taking them to the West Indies. He said that it was a bargain.' Adah sympathised but refused to buy, not even

44

for fifty pence. The man left them, sadly, but not before he warned them that they were missing the chance of a lifetime.

Both women smiled with understanding.

'Poor old man, standing there all day and asking people like me to buy a glass bird. What would I do with a beautiful thing like that? Where would I put it? The dole money will just do to keep me and my five alive. Buy a bird indeed!' said Adah seriously.

'Do you know, I never knew you had five. I have seven,' Mrs O'Brien volunteered, sounding rather tired.

'Wow! Seven! How old are you? Oh, I am sorry, I don't mean to be so inquisitive. But listen, dear, you look too young to be the mother of seven children.'

Mrs O'Brien's laughter was a delight to hear. She was a well-kept and well-preserved woman. Beautiful too, with masses of well-kept fair hair. She wore her hair long, was a little on the plump side, but she had that sort of plumpness which teenagers usually have. She recovered from her laughter and said, 'I'm not very young, thirty-five, and I've buried two kids in Ireland and two here, you know, where we were living before. That was why they had us rehoused. The two died within days of each other. They died of some virus of some sort, meningitis, yea, that was what they called it. Meningitis. That's why I'm so frightened with those gaping chutes. Not just that though; people in the Mansions just won't mind their bleeding business – they talk about other people. They know all about you and just gossip and gossip.'

She came closer to Adah, and lowered her voice as if imparting a state secret. 'You see, my old man is always out of a job, and those nosey parkers think I want him at home on purpose. But that's a lie! He can't get a job. He's a very hard-working man.'

Adah looked at her, not knowing what to say. Everybody at the Mansions knew the O'Brien story. He would not go to work because it did not pay him to work, and here was the O'Brien

45

woman trying to defend the name of her family. What would one call her case, suffering from 'false consciousness' or what? She seemed more sensitive than Adah had imagined.

'Well, you know,' she went on in a tone used by people caught stealing. 'Well, you know, not that he earned much, but he is a good man and would not dream of staying at home just for more money. You know, we're good Catholics, we wouldn't dream of doing a thing like that.'

'A thing like what?' Adah was getting annoyed at this female coward. 'You mean it pays your family more when your husband goes on the dole? Then he would be stupid if he went out to work. Why starve the kids just because of the back-biting neighbours? I would let them talk if I were you. We are not going to stay in the Mansions for ever. We'll soon move to different places, and then you can keep your secret to yourself.'

By now they were in the school compound; they were a bit early and there were all the mums, most of them scarf-wearing, standing in groups waiting patiently for their broods. Mrs O'Brien peered at Adah to see if she was sincere, and apparently something on Adah's face told her she was.

'I always like your people, you are always very frank. I had a Nigerian friend once; she had six children and we used to go to Mass in the same church. She was nice, just like you. She used to tell me not to mind what people say about my children.'

Why was it that everybody would always judge one black person by the way another black person behaved? It never occurred to people like Mrs O'Brien that the other black woman might have come from the Cape of Africa and Adah from the Horn. Or, for that matter, from Trinidad, Boston or even Liverpool or Cardiff.

As long as you're black, any other black person is 'your people'. The bird seller at the Crescent wanted her to buy a bird because one of 'her people', a West Indian, in fact, had bought six the day before. How daft could people be! Too lazy to think.

She nodded her agreement to Mrs O'Brien, not because she

was in the right, but because she sensed that the O'Brien woman was feeling low and was begging for understanding.

'You see, we can just about live on the dole. When he works forty hours a week, he brings home sixteen pound, but when he's on the dole they give us *eighteen* pound, free milk, free vitamin-things for the kids; all the kids at school get free dinners, and sometimes they give us money to buy them shoes. But if Bob goes to work, we lose all that. And yet people talk. I don't know what they want us to do, I just don't know. Oh, Adah, I can't tell you how I feel sometimes, I can't tell you how I feel. It makes me feel ashamed and miserable. Things wouldn't be so bad if he could get somewhere where they'd give him the same amount as we got on the dole. I'm sure he would be very happy to go. But there is nowhere, nobody would employ him for such an amount. Oh, I don't know . . .' Her voice went inaudibly low, tense and tremulous as if it had charged with some vital current and its battery had run down. Her smile was sad and tense. Her plump hands went jerky and shook. She darted her tongue across her lips which had no lipstick and pulled her scarf on properly again. This gesture had a note of final acceptance in it. It seemed to be giving in to Things.

You can't change Things, you just accept them, and in any case the school bell ding-donged them both back to immediate reality.

But Mrs O'Brien's story was infectious. She had closed her mouth like a trap and was readjusting her face for the sake of her kids who would soon be let out of their classroom.

Here was a woman, thought Adah, who would value an honest day's work more than anything. She would be much happier if her husband could earn enough and so, presumably, would he if what she said of him was true, but where did people get a system that allowed a man to be better off when out of work? Adah recalled that people who lived before her generation used to say that diligence was the mother of fortune. Perhaps diligence might still be the mother of fortune for some

47

people. She was puzzled. Probably she could bear her lot more easily because she knew that she could always earn more than she was getting on the dole whenever she decided to go out to work again. But Mrs O'Brien was still better off than she was – she had her man beside her, which was very rare at the Mansions, and she felt compelled to remind Mrs O'Brien of this. She went close to her, so that the other mums could not hear them.

'Look, though, your Bob is nice. Very helpful in the house.'

Mrs O'Brien smiled her thanks. Yes, he was a man in a million, she said. She wouldn't tolerate *any* man around the house all day, but with her Bob, it was different. He was an angel with his kids.

Joy glowed in her eyes. Well, that was something Adah did not understand, the Irish woman was in love with her Bob, even though he did not work for their living – whether gossip was right and he was idle or whether it was really true that he could not earn more than sixteen pounds, he had none the less earned her love and respect; he was no failure in her eyes.

There was no sense in anything anymore. Adah began to feel like being jealous. Perhaps that was why the other women talked. She stopped herself from thinking.

The children rushed out like caged birds suddenly set free. Adah's kids showered her with horrors which they called paintings. There was the usual confusion. Children screaming and mothers shrieking and cooing. Adah's last glimpse of Mrs O'Brien was consoling. Her two grown-up kids were pulling her along by the hand, apparently to Charlie's, the sweet shop. The glimpse was momentary. Adah's own children swarmed around her.

Life might not be as bad as it seemed, not always. Happily they all trooped down to the Mansions. She held the kids' paintings up high as banners to frighten off evil spirits.

7   *The Ministry's Visiting Day*

Adah jumped from her bed to the screams of Mrs Cox.

'Leave that milk alone!' the voice outside shouted.

Adah rushed out of her flat; the little boy had done it again. It was very funny really. The little boy's unwashed face peered at Adah and his little pinkish-white body tried desperately to wriggle out of Mrs Cox's big hand.

'If you steal her milk again, I'll get the law on you,' Mrs Cox howled, and the little boy shrank, his bright eyes gleaming with terror. When she let him go, he dashed blindly into his home. He banged the door so loudly that Mrs Cox and Adah jumped.

'Thank you,' said Adah, as she bent down to pick up her bottles of milk. This was a daily occurrence at the Mansions. If you were late in collecting your bottles of milk in the mornings, they simply disappeared. Nobody sympathised with you when you lost your milk, you just had to keep a good look-out. That was one of the unwritten laws of the Mansions.

'Wake up,' she shouted to her children who were still in bed. Still feeling too lazy to go all the way up, she yelled at the sleeping kids once more.

Just then, there was a clip and a clap from the letter-box. A brown envelope flew down, lifelessly, like a hen's feather. Official sort of envelope. Adah stared at it lazily, guessed that it was from the children's school. The people at that school never had anything good to tell her. Maybe a school officer would be calling on her to tell her that Titi would not eat her baked beans

49

and watery salad. Or that Vicky was bored with his schoolwork the month before. Whatever it was it could wait right there on the mat. She did not want her whole day ruined by some woolly complaints.

She went upstairs quickly. Her two boys had wet their beds. The smell was heavy. Bubu was shivering, his brown, bony, naked body shaking as if doing an African dance. 'You've done it again,' Adah remonstrated.

'Yes, Mum, I was asleep, and I done it,' explained the boy innocently. To him the reason was logical enough, he did it because he was asleep.

'Well, tomorrow try to wake up when you want to do it; after all, there is a potty under your bed. You must learn to use it.'

'Yes, Mum, I would, but it's too cold to get out of bed, and the floor is so cold too.'

Well, what could she say to that? The children had no night clothes. The Ministry would glare if she asked for money to buy night clothes. She was supposed to buy such things from her allowance. She would not blame the kids. She would not blame them about wetting their beds any more. She would just have to live with it. The more one blamed kids for bed-wetting and things, the jumpier they would get. If only she could get enough money to buy them warm clothes, if only she could have enough heating in the bedrooms. Then she remembered the brown envelope on the mat. Carol, the Family Adviser, had promised to write to the Ministry for her, to ask for a shoe allowance. That letter on the mat might be from them. She raced down, with silent prayers on her lips, her heart beating so fast she thought it would burst. She picked up the envelope with shaking hands. Yes, it was from them all right.

'One of my officers will call on you today, the 17th. I am sorry I cannot be more specific about the time.'

'I do wish these people would say what time they would be visiting,' Adah thought. Still, there was now a slight hope that the kids would have decent shoes for the next three months. The night clothes? No, she wouldn't mention those, otherwise the officer would think her greedy. The trouble was that she needed so many things. Bedding, beds, money for the payments on the gas cooker she had foolishly bought when she was working.

'Hurry up,' she sang happily to her children. Happy. The kids would at least have shoes and wellingtons. God bless Carol.

The children had custard for breakfast. There was some rice from the day before, and some of them had that too. Blast balanced meals! You can think of balancing meals when you have enough food. In any case the kids' diet would balance at school all right. For herself, she would pay a visit to Carol and she would be sure of getting a nice strong cup of coffee with milk in it. The milk in the coffee should balance her for the day, or balance her enough till the kids came home from school. Then she would eat more rice. Rice tasted good. It is cheap, it is filling.

She hurried the kids. They dressed quickly. 'Please wait for me, I shan't be long,' read the note she left at her door for the social security officer should he call when she was away. She took the kids to school, grabbed a gallon of paraffin from the owner of the shop down the road. She promised to pay the following week. That was all right – she was an old and well-known customer. She cleaned her flat quickly, dusted the few wooden pieces of furniture, and then lighted the heater with the paraffin she had bought on credit. Get warm now, pay later.

At ten o'clock, she was so hungry that she decided to cook the rice she had kept for the evening. She would just take a few spoonfuls, she promised herself. After all rice made her fat, she should watch her waistline. Well, when the rice was cooked, she forgot about her waistline, she forgot that the portion she cooked was for six. She finished the lot. Anyway that would make her cheerful and alert when the man called. She would go on a diet the following week. She was sure of losing at the very least two whole pounds. Then she would be really beautiful. She would have her bath, she decided. The rice had given her so much energy. The gas meter? Well, next week the Ministry would give her some money for the shoes, so she could afford a luxurious bath while waiting. That would be an extra bath for the week. She only allowed herself three baths a week to save gas. After the bath, she was pleased with herself. She thought she looked and smelt nice. 'At least the officer won't think I'm filthy.'

There was a bang at the door. Oh, it must be him, please God, let it be him. The paraffin made her place a cosy picture, but alas, it was burning low fast. Oh, it was not him. It was Whoopey.

'Hello, Adah,' said Whoopey. She had a squeaky voice, Whoopey had. 'Adah, I have some'nk to tell yer. There are some old clothes just arrived at Carol's. She's only got them this morning. You mustn't miss them, they'll be ever so nice for your kids. I should run and get them now, go on!'

'But I can't,' wailed Adah wringing her hands. 'The almighty Ministry men are descending on me today. I can't leave the house. I might miss them.'

'Are they? I say . . . you do look nice. Just for them? Cor, blimey.'

'Well, since they told me they'd be coming, I thought I'd clean up a bit. You know, just to look nice, you know what I mean.' Adah found herself apologising for having had a bath and put on clean clothes so early in the morning. That was part of living in the ditch. Everybody knew what the other was doing. To have a bath and put on clean clothes was very uncommon. At that time in the morning, when the kids had all gone to school, mums were free to chat on the balconies with bunches of curlers on their heads, old tattered slippers on their feet. You got dressed only when you wanted to take one of 'yours' to see the doctor or the dentist.

'Watch it, those men do take advantage, you know,' said Whoopey nodding her small head vigorously like an African lizard resting in the shade.

'I will be very careful,' promised Adah. She too had heard

funny stories about the social security officers. But at the Mansions, one of the most difficult things to do was to tell what was fantasy and what was fact. Whoopey looked sincere enough, so perhaps there was some truth in them – there might well be.

Whoopey sighed. 'My advice is, don't bother to heat up the sitting-room for them. They'll think you're well off. Why don't you be your age, girl? What do you think you're doing? You're *poor*, let the buggers know you're poor, and that's that. What are the sods coming for, anyway?'

'To give us money for shoes,' replied Adah in a weak voice.

'*Those* lousy men! If your house is warm and you look nice, they'll think you get extra income from God knows where, and may not approve your grant, you know. You have to whine all the time, and make a song and dance of the fact that you're unsupported. The more trouble you make, the more grant you get. If you want to be la-di-da and ladylike with them, you'll get nothing. We are poor, and the bastards want us to look poor. Don't bother yourself at all, and, Adah – good luck. I'll be around in case he makes a grab at you. Just give out a loud yell. You do look nice, I must say. Put ashes on your face and head . . .' Whoopey's voice floated down the balcony.

Adah listened to every sound that came from outside, but no one knocked. One o'clock, and still no social security officer. She was getting hungry again. That was the trouble with being at home and unhappy. You kept wanting to eat all the time. Anyway there was nothing in the house to eat as she still had to do her shopping. She looked at the heater and knew that her paraffin was wasting. What a bloody waste. She was crying now. The man would not come. By three o'clock the social security officers would be drinking their coffee and tea, laughing over the day's experiences. Adah did not like the way the less fortunate were treated. But she would not judge the officers, not really. They expected everyone on the dole to be at home, despite the fact that most of them were women with young children. She had been unable to do her shopping for

53

fear of missing the social security officer, so she had stayed at home and eaten more than she could afford. The paraffin was now low. Wearily, she bent down and turned off the heater. The man might come tomorrow. She would have to borrow another half-a-crown to buy more paraffin for the oil heater. She would probably feel she ought to have another bath too.

She dragged herself out aimlessly on to the balcony, and saw Carol talking to Mrs King in the middle of the compound. Carol looked up and called, 'Come down, Adah, or are you very busy? Do come for coffee!'

'I'll be down right away,' she shouted back, happy to escape from her private gloom.

Living in the ditch had its own consolations and advantages. There were always warm and natural friends. Friends who took delight in flouting society's laws. Some women indulged in having more and more children, a way of making the society that forced them into the ditch suffer. Some enjoyed taking it out on the welfare officers of the Ministry of Social Security, others took to drink. Many women in the ditch found consolation in over-eating. Anything goes, fish and chips and very rich creamy, cheap buns – one of the reasons that explained their distorted figures, with waists and hips like overstuffed pillows.

Adah crossed the compound into Carol's office. All the regulars at Carol's knew of her disappointment. After a few minutes, Adah realised that she was not the first one. Many had had similar experiences. Well, it was consoling to note that many had shared a misfortune like hers.

'Cheer up, Adah,' consoled Carol. 'I'll phone them right now.'

Carol did telephone, and the officer who answered promised to look into it. Yes, the officer would look into it, while the likes of Adah – separated mums, old-age pensioners, and the very poor – waited in the ditch biting their nails.

8 *The Ditch-Dwellers*

Adah was busy mending some of the clothes she got from the clothes exchange when her wandering thoughts were suddenly disturbed by an ear-shattering noise. The noise was too penetrating to be one of the ordinary daily noises. She walked out on to the balcony and saw children in colourful summer clothes gathered by the door of Number X. Mums and dads from the top balconies popped their heads out to watch fair play. It was the King family. They were at it again. The usual fight.

'Go away, you bloody good-for-nothing fool! I've no need of yer, so don't ever come bloody back again.'

Mrs King was yelling at her husband, her voice croaking and a kind of foam gathered round her twitching mouth. Adah tiptoed up like someone possessed.

Anger had really taken hold of Mrs King.

'I have no need of yer, I got the flat from the Council in me own name, so sod off to the bloody pubs and drink 'oles into your mother's bottom!'

The listening kids cheered, though what Mrs King meant by the last statement was ambiguous, even to the watching grown-ups.

'If I get 'old of yer, you bitch . . .!' growled back her husband, a dirty, rough man of uncertain age. He stood with legs apart, clutching a bit of dirty clothing in his wet mouth. His head was bent in concentration. He was pre-occupied with his trousers, trying to do something to them. The trousers would not stay round his waist. Eventually he got the piece of clothing from his mouth and strung it through some holes in the upper part and tied them round his waist securely. Thus equipped, he was ready to face his wife. He charged in like a bull thundering at the door, demanding admittance. Mrs King had the door securely locked. Their seven children stood outside, watching, unhappy. They all looked cold even though the evening was warm. The baby clung to the big sister. Their mother was in no state to hold him.

'She's always going on like that at 'er ol' man, you know.' This came from an old lady who had witnessed it all. She was talking to Adah and a group of unhappy people who were watching, helpless, unable to do anything. 'She's a bitch. A dirty ol' bitch; a bloody ol' bag too,' she added, raising her voice. No one responded.

'You never done a single 'onest day's job in yer 'ole life. You rotten, rotten fool. If you bang at that door again, I'll get the law on yer,' Mrs King threatened.

Mr King was not the sort of person to fear the law. The police could do little for a beaten wife. Sometimes it seemed that matrimony, apart from being a way of getting free sex when men felt like it, was also a legalised way of committing assault and getting away with it.

Mr King said by way of explanation, 'She wants me out of the way so that she can bring in her fancy men and collect large sums of money from the Ministry of Social Security.'

'Yeah, go, and say what you like. I'm not having you here any more. You give me ten pounds to feed us nine, pay for yer bloody fags and yer stinking drinks. Oh, no, I'm fed up with yer.' Mrs King broke down and started to cry. Everybody was sorry for her. But that was the living pattern at the Mansions – and many felt sorry for Mr King too.

Mr King, tired, sat on the steps in front of his flat. He had stopped arguing. His children looked at him in shame, mixed

56

with horror. They looked as if they were more in sympathy with their mother than their father. One of the boys drifted away to his friends. Mrs King poked her head out of the front window, saw her husband, and drew her head back in. The head came out a second later, this time her hand shot out as well. She was carrying a red plastic pail. She quickly poured the contents on the head of her unsuspecting husband as if baptising him. She didn't want him sitting there. Mr King made a blind dash for her but his wife knew him very well and was just too quick for him. She banged the window shut. Mrs King had looked as if she was crying. Only God knew what would have happened to her that evening if her husband could lay his hands on her. He banged on the door, this time with the intention of breaking it open. He used both his elbows, his head and feet. The door was about to give way when one of his sons, guessing what the fate of their mother would be, threw a broken beer bottle at him and ran. Mr King's head started to bleed. He guessed that he was fighting a losing battle. He held his head in both his hands, like the picture of the convict in *Great Expectations*, and limped away, leaving a trail of blood behind him.

Thus did Mrs King join the rest of the fatherless families. Perhaps she would not have joined them if she and her husband had been living somewhere else, but here at the Mansions she saw fatherless families who were much better off. Those at the top could afford to talk about love. Surely, they would admonish, these families should love one another: wives, after all, marry for better and for worse and they should not forget it. Well, many wives at the Pussy did remember all right. But when the family was a large one, and the husband could not earn enough to keep them out of poverty, and to cap it all, took it upon himself to bring home only part of his income – then the original love was bound to die. Love is like a living thing. It has to be fed, nurtured and even pampered to weather time. How many middle-class women would welcome a penniless, drunkard pouncing on her in bed, just like an animal, simply because he married her?

Mr King left the Pussy reluctantly, and a sad man. He never came back again. When, months later, everybody at the Pussy was being rehoused, the King family left, without Mr King.

When the noise had subsided, Mrs Ashley, who had been watching, turned away to go back to her flat. 'Oh, never mind the Kings,' she said turning to Adah. 'The husband is no good, he drinks all the time. Don't mind them, my dear, some men are bad and selfish. Look, mine does *not* want me to look nice. Whenever I have me hair done he gets red all over. It's wickedness, that's what I call it. Well, my dear, nobody wants these flats any more,' went on Mrs Ashley, quickly changing the subject of the conversation, 'they are bad for the health and the spirit. We all want to move out, and we've been at it for years. The tenants have paid the Council double the amount it took them to build them. I should advise you to come and join the Tenants' Association. We meet on Mondays and there we discuss what's to happen. We can't go on like this.' She stopped abruptly, waiting to see if Adah was with her. She slapped her face mistakenly in an attempt to frighten off a buzzing fly.

Adah agreed to join and that made Mrs Ashley very happy.

The crowd at the King family's door started to move unwillingly away in search of some other amusement. Mrs Murray saw Adah and Mrs Ashley standing together, so she walked over for a chat. Mrs Murray was a widow, a skinny, ill-looking widow with masses of old clothes and worn-out slippers. She had a way with her teeth, which made her rather unique. Her nickname was 'the Princess'. She had once been a very beautiful woman, but a good part of her died with her husband. His death smashed her up completely, like Humpty Dumpty, so much so that no amount of sympathy and socialising would make her pick herself up again. She limped along the balcony to where the Ashley woman and Adah were discussing the Kings.

'He's no good, that man. It was her fault, though. She let him give her babies and allowed him to drink. Well, he didn't know when to stop,' the Princess volunteered, staring from Mrs Ashley to Adah, quite unsure whether she had scored a point or not. Mrs Ashley as usual was nodding in agreement. The mass of red locks of hair on her head danced happily. The Princess relapsed into silence. Her limping walk towards them, and her little speech, had exhausted her. She took a hairpin from her hair and started to pick her teeth again. She was not naturally a good conversationalist but was very good nevertheless at starting a conversation. Mrs Ashley took up the thread, and they discussed all the discussables about the Kings, and finished up with the pathetic story of the Princess and her husband who had died ten years before. The Princess hung her head to one side like a martyr. She was enjoying the pity. That made her even more pitiable.

'I went to the court yesterday,' she declared, all of a sudden.

'Oh? Whatever for? Are you in trouble of some sort?' Mrs Ashley urged.

'Well, the Assistance Board took me to court. They wanted to know why it was that I took up a cleaning job without declaring the amount.'

'Those people are wicked!' said Mrs Ashley, nudging Adah in the ribs. To the Ashley woman, people were either her 'dears' or they were wicked. She seemed capable of using only those two adjectives to describe all her feelings about people.

'They said to me, "Aren't yer better off than when your husband was alive?" '

'Ah, that was really a wicked thing to say,' put in Adah, borrowing Mrs Ashley's favourite adjective. 'After all you did not kill him, did you? You could not have killed him just to live on their money! They have no feelings, these stiffnecked bureaucrats.' Adah, forgetting that she was in England, spat on the floor, as the people of her tribe would do when they talked of anything they thought was obnoxious.

'I never killed nobody. Their million pounds cannot replace me Toby. They don't know what they're talking about, those

59

men,' the Princess went on tearfully while Mrs Ashley shook her head, and said, 'Wicked, wicked,' intermittently.

'The magistrate was more human, though. He said to me, "Go away and don't repeat it," as if I can with this bleeding foot.'

'I noticed you limping; what is the matter with your foot?' asked Adah.

'It 'urts. I 'ave to wear trousers most of the time and I can't show me legs to fancy men,' the Princess regretted.

'Wow,' shouted Mrs Ashley. 'I didn't know you had a fancy man!'

'You'd be surprised. I had a date the other day.'

Adah and Mrs Ashley believed her. After all, the Princess was not an ugly woman, just a simple soul begging for sympathy.

There were all sorts of stories going on at the Pussy Cat Mansions about fancy men. Separated women were not allowed to have 'fancy men', the phrase for men friends. If a woman was regularly seen with one, she'd had it. The dole people would want to know if the fancy man would help with the support of the woman and if so by how much, so that it could be deducted from her weekly dole. Of course, they usually drove the fancy men away. The women not only had to be poor, but they had to be sex-starved too. Their chances of marrying or remarrying were reduced almost to nil.

The social argument was that if any of these women were allowed to have sex with their men friends, there would always be unwanted babies, and they would probably then have a double income, one from the fancy men, the other from the Dole House. Well, that may have been true. What of the morals of a middle-class secretary in an office, and who complained about so-called personal secretaries and private nurses? Did they not receive gifts from the makers of the System whom they worked for? The trouble with the System on this issue was that no one knew where the definition of respectable spinster ended and that of prostitute began. Also, with the popularity of the

Pill, the diaphragm, contraceptive jelly and free abortion, how could it be necessary for society to be so inhuman? To most of these women sex was like food. Love was dead, except the maternal love they had naturally for their kids. To be deprived sexually, especially for women in their twenties who had once been married, was probably one of the reasons why places like the Pussy Cat Mansions were usually a fertile ground for breeding hooligans and generations of unmarried mums.

The little group talked, gossiped and laughed; all were happy. They found joy in communal sorrow. Children ran between their legs, happy at the knowledge of the nearness of their mothers. Adah stopped being homesick. She was beginning to feel like a human being again with a definite role to perform – even though the role was in no other place but the ditch. It was always nice and warm in the ditch.

That night she thanked God for her good neighbours.

9 *It's Dole Day*

That day was a Monday. Right from her childhood, Adah had hated Mondays. The fact that it had been raining the night before did not improve the situation. Lazily she put out her hand from under layers and layers of old discarded blankets, handed down to her by Carol. Only God knew where Carol got them. She drew a circle on the wall with one of her fingers, and water oozed out from it. As usual with the Pussy Cat Mansions, it rained inside as well as outside on damp days. She prayed the children would not wake up as early as she had. She shrank far, far deeper into her warm bed.

Her prayers were too late. 'Mummy, I woke first.' One of her little girls was up already. Why can't kids wait until they are called?

'Mummy, wake up! It is morning,' repeated Dada, her voice urgent and impatient.

'All right, I shan't be a minute, darling.' This was too late as the little girl was in her room already. She had on an old man's jumper. The jumper was grey, torn and full of holes. But it was warm, which was why Adah had taken it from the clothes exchange in the first place. It was too long for the child, so to add glamour and beauty to it, Adah had belted the middle with an old red granddad tie. Sometimes she used to wonder about the people who had once owned all the old clothes. To ease her conscience, she usually had them boiled before giving them to the children.

'Say good-morning to Mummy.'

'Good morning, Mummy,' the little girl sang. 'I did not wet my bed today. See, Mummy, see, I did not wet my bed.'

'Very good, that's very good,' said Adah getting up, since she had no choice. She would have liked to stay in bed longer.

'Where is my sixpence?' asked the girl.

'What sixpence, what do you want a sixpence for so early in the morning?' said Adah, turning from the bed she was making to look at her daughter.

'You said you'd give me a sixpence if I did not wet my bed. You said, yes, you did. You did, Mum.' The girl's voice was quaking dangerously with the beginning of a cry. Adah could not stand that so early in the morning.

'But I only promised to give you a sixpenny bit for your tooth. I don't remember my promising to give you anything when you are dry in bed. But I'll think about it. If you are good, you'll have it.'

'Oh,' the girl's voice wobbled as dangerously as ever. She gave up talking and started a low whining cry.

'I promise. I'll give you the sixpenny bit when you come back from school. But if you cry you'll forfeit your money.'

'What's forfeit? What's forfeit, Mum?'

'Never mind, some other time. Run along upstairs. I'll come soon to give you a wash, then you'll be nice and clean for school.'

Pacified, the little girl ran upstairs, shouting her triumph to the others. 'I am having a sixpence today. I am having a sixpence today.'

'So what?' Titi's voice cut in from their bedroom.

The bang at the door announced the arrival of the milkman. Adah had told him to give a loud knock whenever he delivered the milk, so that she would not put temptation in the way of the milk pinchers. She threw her lappa around her and ran out. The little boy from No. X who usually pinched her milk, saw her come out, and knowing that he had lost his bounty for the day, gave Adah an innocent smile and withdrew into his home just for a second. His blond head shot out again followed by another baby smile. To him it was just like playing hide-and-seek. Adah smiled back, happy that he had not been given another chance to be a little thief. Turning back to her door, she realised that the black dog from No. X was waiting impatiently for her to go in. The dog wanted to deposit its morning droppings.

'Go away, you idiot,' she blazed at the dog, having made sure that three-quarters of her body was safely inside her flat. 'Go away, do you hear? Go and do that at your own door. Why do you have to come here anyway? Go *away*.' The dog seemed to be thinking, for it looked at Adah sympathetically. Unfortunately, the call of nature was imminent and pressing. The dog did not move an inch. It simply stared uncomprehending.

The big lady from next door wobbled out at the sound of Adah's pathetic voice. She had on a baggy old house-coat, the colour of which was completely faded. Strands of hair hung loose round her face like wet feathers. She clutched an old worn-out mop in her big masculine hands, and thundered at the dog with her mighty voice, poking at it with the filthy mop. The dog, disgusted, took to its heels and ran. Mrs Cox opened her little mouth and laughed, the morning saliva in her unwashed mouth bubbling merrily. Adah joined in the laughter, amused and thankful.

'You must get a big mop like mine,' boasted Mrs Cox. 'It frightens them damned dogs. Eeyer, do you know that you are not supposed to own dogs in these bleeding holes? But nobody cares for this fucking old place. People just do what they like. The bleeding bastards.'

'Yes, I know, but what I fail to understand is that the dog chooses my door to other places. I wouldn't mind if it went somewhere else, I wouldn't mind at all.'

'You're near the chute, that's why. That was why the tenants who were living there before you moved away. The chute, it smells 'orribly. Tell them to do some'ink about it. I would hold the rent, I would.'

They both laughed, because at the Pussy Cat Mansions, withholding the rent was the only weapon the tenants had. The council officers would threaten to evict the tenant, but they usually gave in, for who else, except perhaps squatters, would live in the vacant Pussy flats?

Mrs Cox was always in a good talking mood; seven o'clock was not too early for her. She was just ready for a good old chat at that time of the morning. Unfortunately, Adah had to get her kids ready for school. 'Yes, dear, I'm coming,' Adah shouted at her door to give her kindly neighbour the idea that one of her kids was calling her. She quickly bolted into her flat, before Mrs Cox could have time to realise she had been deceived.

Mrs Cox was a dear soul, but a disappointed woman. She had lived at the Pussy Cat Mansions 'all her life since the War'. Adah did not always know which war. Everybody was always saying 'since the War'. Whether it was the last war, or the one before that, or another one before that, she never bothered to find out. Mrs Cox looked sixty, but she heard the Family Adviser say on one occasion that Mrs Cox was only forty-nine. Her figure, if one could call it that, had been irrevocably distorted by either too much work, or bad food, or by frequent child-bearing. There was no demarcation between her bust, waist and hips. All together they formed one huge cylindrical block. Her kids were all grown-up. The girls were all with her, with their own babies. One of the girls was once married, but came back to 'Mum' as Fred was 'inside'. The other had three coloured children and since she did not want to lose her respectability, she came back to 'Mum'. Mrs Cox became the 'Mum' for everybody. Sometimes more than a mum and more of a working-class Wise Woman, like Ena Sharples is to T.V.'s 'Coronation Street'. Mrs Cox also reminded Adah of most African matrons – you don't ask them to help you, they just do it. They, like Mrs Cox, have that sense of mutual help that is ingrained in people who have known a communal rather than an individualistic way of life.

Inside Adah's flat, her kids were at breakfast. 'Are we having eggs for breakfast tomorrow?' asked Bubu, heaving a sigh of boredom at the big bowl of cornflakes in front of him.

'Yes, dear, I'll go to the post office this morning and get some money, buy the eggs at the Crescent, and then you can have them for tomorrow. But for the time being, finish those cornflakes. They're good for you. Think of all those children in Biafra!'

'Here we go again,' put in Titi, Adah's biggest girl.

'Well, it's true, isn't it? Would you like to go to Biafra?'

'Why should I go to Biafra? I don't even know where it is. And I don't want to go. So!'

Adah looked thoughtfully at this six-year-old, who thought she knew everything. The funniest thing was that she was not afraid of speaking her mind, not even to her mum. She had tried to paint rosy pictures of Nigeria to her kids, the graceful palm trees, coconut-lemonade and all that, yet they were only curious, not really moved. They made Adah feel so old, as if she was talking of another world rather than a place which she left only a few years before. 'Don't tell them at school,' she said. 'Don't tell them you are not proud of your country.'

'When I grow up, I'll choose my country, but not now,' was Titi's snap answer.

'I don't think I'm going to like the eggs tomorrow,' said Bubu changing his little mind. 'I think I'd like to have sweets today instead.'

'Well, you can't have sweets for breakfast, nobody does,' said Adah.

'Some of my friends do,' put in Vicky. 'Some even have chips.'

Children can be so illogical, Adah thought, but knew it was time to discontinue the argument. She would never win anyway. What was the point?

All of a sudden Bubu stretched and upset the cornflakes bowl. The soaked cornflakes looked pathetic, like damp autumn leaves. Adah was cross. She lifted Bubu from his wet chair and gave him two hot smacks on his bottom. Blast Dr

66

Spock or whoever it was that was preaching overpermissiveness with children! One could let kids have their own way when you had only one or two and in an ideal home with an ideal film-star-like husband, who would be ready to bring home pots and pots of money, Adah thought to herself. 'That will teach you. Cornflakes cost money. A lot of money.'

The kids behaved very well for the rest of the morning. *I'm sure they will grow to hate me, these kids*, she decided miserably. *I wish I could control my temper. Anyway, Bubu is only four, he'll forget by the time he grows up. I can't be hated by all five of them. Was it not Jesus who said that only one cured leper came back to say thank you, after ten had been cured? Well, I'm not going to have ten kids to be sure of one thankful one. I'll give them the best I can and no more. I am not going to indulge them in having sweets for breakfast, so that I may be remembered in old age. Sweets are bad for teeth.*

'You know don't you, that sweets are bad for your teeth. You don't want to start going to a dentist before you are old, do you? Look at my teeth. I've never been to a dentist, and they are perfect. You know why? I never had sweets when I was your age,' Adah said, trying to console herself.

Titi burst out laughing.

'What's funny?'

'Nothing, I just wondered whether there were any sweet shops when you were little, in Africa.'

'Shut your dirty mouth,' shouted Vicky, fed up with the whole show.

Adah boiled a kettle of water, and took it to the bathroom. The hot-water system provided took such a long time to get started that it was always quicker and safer to boil one's water at the Mansions. The kids washed themselves and Adah took them to school.

The post office was at Queen's Crescent. The queue had reached the post office box outside. There were many people on the dole, on supplementary benefits and on all sorts of benefits. Most of them collected their money on Mondays.

'Ad, come here, jump the queue.' It was Whoopey, Mrs Cox's daughter.

'You can't do that!' shouted the post office clerk.

'Oh, shut your bleeding trap and get on with your work,' Whoopey shouted, her voice squeaking.

The arguments and obscenities that followed made the poor man work harder. The quarrel was not a serious one, for everyone knew squeaky-voiced Whoopey. They collected their money and went to queue again at the Rent Office. Whoopey became impatient.

'I'd like to keep the money and let them come for it, I would. I hate this bleeding wait.'

'It's a nuisance,' agreed Adah, 'but I have to complain about those dogs, so I'll have to wait.'

'I'm waiting then, with you. You don't shout loud enough, that's your trouble. I'll do the shouting for you. Those dogs must be stopped.' Whoopey lit her cigarette and smoked nervously, her sharp piercing eyes watchful.

Whoopey was so unlike her mother. She was small, restless and fidgety. Her mind too was capable of switching from one topic to another, just like one would change from one station to another on a radio. She wrinkled her brow. She was thinking. She nudged Adah.

'Have the Ministry called on you yet? You waited for them the other day. It was such a shame.'

Adah detected a note of suppressed humour in Whoopey's voice. She remembered her advice to her that day. 'Don't clean up for them, they don't deserve it.' She smiled pleasantly, remembering that the money was still to come. 'No, they are still looking into it,' she replied.

'Yes, I know, sometimes it takes a long time to look into it. It took them a bleeding three months looking into the fact that I needed a bed to sleep on once. I was mad. Move over, lover.'

The last remark was made to a startled old man who was so surprised at being called 'lover' that his knees shook visibly.

Whoopey laughed, and nudged Adah in the ribs. 'I bet he thinks I fancy him, poor feller.'

'I am sure he has forgotten how to perform in bed. You should go and teach him, but make sure you've got his pension money in your purse first, poor feller,' finished Adah.

They went on chatting blatant nothings to kill time, and to make them forget the fact that the queue was slow in moving. Eventually Whoopey handed in her rent card.

'How much are you paying this week?' the clerk asked, his face turned to Whoopey, who was puffing at the tiny end of a burnt-out cigarette. Apparently there was some rent in arrears. Whoopey did not like to be asked that way, not when there were others watching. Her annoyance showed in the way she was puffing and breathing and deliberately causing delay.

'How much are you paying this week?' the clerk asked, his voice raised a little, betraying the fact that he too was losing his temper. He was making a mistake, to lose his temper with the likes of Whoopey, because it was temper wasted. She would enjoy it.

'All right, who said I was deaf? Four pounds. Light my fag for us, please,' she said to another Pussy Cat tenant who was standing almost at the end of the queue. Her fag alight, she came back to her position.

The clerk was still gaping at her. 'You can't just pay four pounds, it's not even up to a week's rent, to say nothing of the a—'

'I know, give over,' Whoopey drawled. 'If you don't take that four pounds, you won't see it again. I'll go and spend it, and there will be nothing for you to take from me and I'll tell them at the Town 'all that you refused the money. You better take it and just mind your bleeding business, the arrears is my own affair, it has nothing to do with you. Okay?' It was pointless arguing with Whoopey. Before the clerk could recover, she switched to another topic.

'Adah's door is being used by them flipping dogs as toilets. Tell 'im. Tell 'im!' Whoopey gave Adah a gentle push.

69

The poor clerk looked from Whoopey to Adah and back again to Whoopey. Lastly he glanced at the now elongated queue and sighed. He removed his glasses, moistened his dry lips and asked Adah, 'Where is your rent?'

Adah became bold too. Oh, no, she was not going to pay her rent if nothing was going to be done about those irresponsible dogs. 'Actually I came to report the droppings. It is very unpleasant.' Trouble with Adah was that she could never speak good London English, or cockney. Her accent and words always betrayed the fact that she had learned her English via *English for Foreign Students*.

'Well, I know about the dogs, but let's get the rent paid for a start,' said the clerk in a caressingly low voice.

Adah was moved. She stretched out her hand to give him the money but the Mansions' tenant who had previously lit Whoopey's fag dashed from the back, and held back Adah's hand.

'Oh, no, she's not paying your flipping rent,' broke in a new voice. 'Do some'ink about them bleeding bitches, first. You told me the other day that our Billy was not allowed to keep his poor dog wot's clean as a ha'pence. Why are you quiet about these right filthy mongrels? Say some'ink!'

Oh, God, vendetta, solidarity, which?

'Yes, I know, but why don't you let Mrs er . . . er . . . speak for herself?' Feet started to shuffle at the back of the queue. The man behind Adah was busy reading on a poster about the blood donors who saved the life of a mum. The mum was grinning from ear to ear, surrounded by children who were so well dressed that it was a perfect picture of a happy family. The interesting thing was that the husband was happy too. Perhaps he had just realised the value of his wife.

'I have to go back to work, you know,' the man announced.

He was completely ignored, especially as his eyes did not leave the blood donor's picture.

The hum of irritated voices died down a little and Adah found her tongue. She always felt insecure, uncertain and

70

afraid. It is a curse to be an orphan, a double curse to be a black one in a white country, an unforgivable calamity to be a woman with five kids but without a husband. Her whole life had been like that of a perpetually unlucky gambler. Every fool of a woman can keep a man; she could not even do that. She had so many chips on her shoulder, and her trouble was that she had only two shoulders on which to carry them; but, luckily, at the Pussy Cat Manions there was always a warm chat, a nice cup of tea and solidarity against any foe. She felt strong, and even crossed her arms akimbo and threw her tightly-scarved head back. *It's a free country*, her attitude seemed to say. But one piercing glare from the clerk cut her down to size. Whoopey and Billy's mum did not see the glare, and even if they had seen it, would have only said, 'What are you staring at me like that for? You look like a dead goat.' But with Adah it was different. She interpreted every glance differently, even when the glance was innocent. She had been nicely conditioned by rejection. She quickly lowered her eyes, and tried to explain apologetically.

'You see, these dogs always do their toilets at my door. It's so embarrassing . . . it smells. Worse when it rains.'

'Embarer – what?' shouted Billy's mum. 'Don't give him that nice talk. Do some'ink, that's what I say. I don't know nothing about all that nice stuff. If you don't do nothing, then don't ask for the rent. Come on, Adah, we'll go to the pub and spend it, won't we?' Billy's mum was really getting her own back.

The other clerks had now stopped work and simply stared at the two white women with a black one sandwiched in between like a good sponge cake. Differences in culture, colour, backgrounds and God knows what else had all been submerged in the face of greater enemies – poverty and helplessness.

The female clerks looked at them, but knew better than to say anything. One of them brought 'the book'. 'The book' was a red tattered register-like affair into which anything about council housing in that part of Camden was scribbled. If one's windows were broken by young thugs, it was scribbled in 'the

71

book'. If you pushed the rent collector away from your door – or even down the stairs – it was written in 'the book'. 'The book' had the look of the register of death, the end of it all.

The male clerk scribbled in 'the book', but a little too quickly and too willingly for the watchful eyes of Whoopey. 'I've taken note of it. The Mayor will come to see you today about your dog.'

'Oh, you bleeding liar, she wants no bloody mayor, and she has no flipping dog and don't lie to me, you've written nothing about it down. We are not moving from here until you do,' Whoopey said triumphantly.

'Oh, for goodness' sake,' put in one of the female clerks in a middle-class accent.

'Shut your trap, you sex-starved buffalo,' someone snapped.

'What's Adah's number? Tell me what her number is,' Whoopey rejoined.

'Oh, I forgot to put *that* down,' replied the clerk.

'You see, you didn't write anything down,' asserted Whoopey. 'Now be a good boy and write it all down,' she went on with mock gentleness.

The clerk patiently started right from the beginning, and every detail was put down, and he even thanked the 'ladies' for their co-operation.

Everybody laughed. Adah always liked the way most quarrels ended happily.

Weeks later, she wondered whether it was worth all the trouble. She saw no mayor, and the dogs continued to leave their droppings outside her door, sometimes bringing their friends from the Prince of Wales Road. Pussy Cat Mansions were just made like that. Very difficult to change anything.

10 *Christmas is Coming*

Christmas was in the air. The kids at the Mansions attended different charity Christmas parties. Adah's came home from most of them loaded with cheap plastic toys which nobody wanted. Somebody at the Children's Department was inspired by a noble idea. Mums from the ditch were to come together with their kids to be given a taste of real life. A spacious hall was chosen, it was cleaned, well-heated and brightly decorated. The festivities were to last a whole week – the week preceding Christmas. Free meals were to be given to mothers and their children. Free toys were also provided, and children were to be encouraged to take away as many as possible.

The idea was smashing. Carol used her car as a taxi. She took kids from the Pussy Cat Mansions to the hall and back again. There was music, children ate, danced and played. Mothers talked and everybody jollied. The happiest part of it was that mothers were not called upon to help with the washing-up. They were just to sit down, have a rest, and, for that particular week, drown their sorrows in being treated like ladies.

'This is nice,' the Princess declared. 'Me walls are unbearable in this weather. They weep like, like widows . . . cor, me rotten food cupboard is all gone green.' She would not be the Pussy Princess if she could forget her woes. Whining and moaning was so much part of her life that she was by now incapable of any other kind of conversation. This time, however, she was ignored for some time because most of the women were determined to be happy: no one wanted to be reminded of damp walls when they were all sitting comfortably in a dry, well-heated hall.

The Princess went on and on about how her two children had to share her bed, because theirs was wet with damp. Adah was sorry for her but had become hardened into impatience; she was sorry for herself too.

'Oh, well, we'll all move soon,' she said. Secretly, the possibility of a move was clouded by misgivings. There was a mixture of scepticism and a determination not to build on false hopes, but at the back of this was, she had to admit, fear. She was not at all sure that she *wanted* to be rehoused yet, not at all sure that she was ready to face the world without the warm, human comfort of the Pussy crowd. Were the damp wet walls of the Mansions any worse than fine dry walls of a new council flat in Godknowswhere if she was to be enclosed in them without friends to support and amuse her? Would better-off, working-class neighbours try to humiliate her because she was black? Could she be black and proud when she had so little of which to be proud *except* her race and her children? So, she made her statement more to sound out public opinion than to assert her hopes or beliefs. She soon found she was not alone in her thoughts.

'I wouldn't like to move too far from me mum,' said Whoopey, who was standing behind Adah. Adah wondered why she was standing, when every mum was given a chair to sit down, but Whoopey could never relax. She was, as usual, holding a cigarette in her right hand. A faded apron was tightly tied round her waist. No one knew why she did that; after all, mums were not going to do any washing-up. But Whoopey would never be complete without an apron and a cigarette, which always seemed to be out. Holding her cigarette in the air like that gave Whoopey confidence. 'Because, you see, me little girl would be bloody sick, without me mum,' she added finally.

74

'Never mind about that . . . I'll keep an eye on yer, even if I'm living on the bloody moon,' Mrs Cox shouted from the other end of the hall. This announcement was followed by one of her loud and explosive laughs. Her laughter was always so spontaneous, and sometimes unexpected, that invariably it was effective. The other listening mums joined in with giggles.

Young men and women from Task Force were busily engaged in arranging tables and laying places for dinner. All of a sudden there was a fight in which one of Adah's five kids was involved. Bubu was Adah's third child. He was always a bit difficult. He had a way of getting into trouble and a way of explaining his behaviour so plausibly afterwards that one could only feel astonishment that all the little things which happened were never, under any circumstances, his fault. Before leaving home that morning Adah had begged all of them to be on good behaviour: to remember to say their pleases and little thank-yous. Bubu had apparently been carried away by the excitement, but Adah was frightened, for the other boy's head seemed to be bleeding badly – Bubu had thrown a toy at him. She was usually a strict mother, but not a self-confident one. To demonstrate confidence and control over her boys she gripped her little son by the collar, shook him and boxed his ears. Then she looked round for approval. She was anxious to take the right attitude in such a situation, to follow her own instincts as a mother and yet to fit in with accepted ideas so that people would not talk.

A youth from Task Force walked up to her and said, 'It was not his fault. Robert threw the tractor at your Bubu. He dodged it, and Robert fell. I saw it happen.' Adah was ashamed but greatly mollified. As a person she did not believe in showing such a wild temper in public, but she had to do something to allay the impression that her children were always allowed to have their own way. She let go of Bubu and walked back to the mums. No one said anything to her and she felt like a child who had been caught showing off. That was one of her problems, she could never be herself. She was always frightened that her

75

real self was not good enough for the public. She would gladly play any role expected of her for the sake of peace.

The talk of moving was predominant because it was winter when the Mansions were at their worst; the cost of keeping the Pussy flats warm was high, and many tenants had to go short on food to pay for warmth.

Like most immigrants in London, Adah heated her flat with paraffin. She had tried coalite, but it proved too expensive, too difficult to light and, moreover, only two of her five rooms had fireplaces. She could move her lighted heater to the bathroom when giving the children their weekly baths. Many poor people, immigrant or otherwise, heated their flats in this way even though most were well aware of the danger. The danger came home to Adah one night when she was sitting watching the dreamy ladies of Peyton Place on her flickering second-hand television very late at night.

'Mummy, oh, Mummy,' came the cry from Dada.

Adah decided to ignore her. After running round them the whole day, she always looked forward to a quiet evening with cosy, undemanding television programmes. 'She's probably dreaming,' she said to herself, relaxing in her chair. But the cry was repeated; it was a choking sort of cry, that of someone in real agony.

She ran up and was stunned by what she found. She could hardly get into the babies' room. It was full of thick smoke. The blanket that covered them was actually on fire and the others were badly scorched. Bubu had had enough sense to shout, but not sense enough to get up or wake her little sister, who funnily enough was sleeping through the noise. Probably she was enjoying the heat. Adah snatched her babies, put them in safety, and covered the burning paraffin heater with what was left of the blanket. Smoke choked her and she coughed, rather painfully, because the smoke was already filtering into her lungs. She was too scared to shout for help. People would only say 'We told you so', and she thought she could do without such chastisement. Luckily the fire went out. Bubu had shouted just in time. Thousands of terrifying thoughts raced through her mind. *Suppose I had been asleep. Suppose I had been out, or suppose Dada was a deep sleeper! Oh, my poor kids, my poor, poor kids.* She held them to her heart, almost crushing them. The baby, now afraid, cried with fear, wondering perhaps at her mother's behaviour.

The heater was a new one, but the children had broken the flimsy glass protection that was built into it to make it air-proof. Adah could not afford to replace the glassy stuff, so she had risked lighting it without protection. The window had been left half open, and the wind came in through the window and fanned the open fire. She was lucky to have her children alive, she knew, and was deeply thankful. She took the frightened kids into her room and wrapped them up in her own blankets. Three of them shared her single bed for months. There was no money for new blankets (naturally no one in the Mansions could afford insurance) and she would not go through the ordeal of answering the uncomfortable personal questions of the social security men again. To tell Carol was out of the question. She knew the reply: 'I told you not to heat your flat with those things, they are dangerous.' *But what does she want me to heat my flat with? I can't afford any other type of heating.*

The trouble with living on the dole is that provision is rarely made for such upheavals. Even where entitlements exist, people who need them seldom know of their existence. Adah, like many others in the ditch, just had to drift along 'making-do'.

She needed a new heater, new blankets, Christmas presents for the kids. Like every other mother, she wanted to give presents to her own children. She would have liked them to have gifts chosen by herself, bought with her own money, rather than the rich man's cast-off toys, or badly made ones which big stores were sure would not sell, so gave away to charities. This wasn't ingratitude, but sound commonsense. Was it too much to ask? she argued with herself. She did not feel like applying for grants just for the kids' Christmas

77

presents. *I want to give my children my own presents, what I actually work for. I don't want my dignity as a person denied me, I must do something.* Ideas came to her head. She was still young, and with a rather Cleopatra type of prettiness. Square face, and determined chin, not the classical European type, nor the typical African beauty. Deep, luminous and rather large eyes gave her face a maiden-in-distress look. Her long stay in the ditch had taught her how best to make those eyes talk. That was a blessing, because her thick full lips always said the wrong things anyway. Eye-rolling was a safer way.

The trouble was, she thought, she was not slim any more; five children took their toll of any girl's figure. Her face had gradually become bloated, the squareness was being gradually covered up by fatty flesh. So, any glamour job was out of the question.

11 Charring for Christmas

'I must look for a part-time job. After all, I'm entitled to earn another couple of pounds a week without losing my dole money. The supplementary benefit laws allow me that.'

The employment agency in Kentish Town Road wanted only typists and full-timers, not students as Adah styled herself. Walking down Holmes Road she saw an advertisement outside a factory. They wanted a cleaner. She asked herself again and again whether to go for it or not. She walked round the factory twice, and on the third time marched in.

The door opened into a clean and simply furnished room. There were two chattering office girls at one end. The two girls, surprisingly, did not keep her waiting for long. One of them, a plump one with a happy smile, came to her and asked her what she wanted. Cleaning job, yes, of course, she was to wait until the guv'nor was free. A chair was shown to her with another flash of the happy smile and she was abandoned.

The two girls went on with their conversation. They were not very fortunate though, because they were constantly interrupted by endless telephone calls from somewhere or other in the factory. Every two minutes or so, someone had to be put through to some section or to some other person. Adah busied her mind with these calls, and was thinking that that sort of job must be great. The thin girl had a typewriter in front of her, her fingers occasionally brushed the keys while the plump one answered the phone calls. The thin girl probably had something to type, but Adah noted that she did not type a single letter for the whole twenty minutes or so that she sat there.

There was another call; this was apparently from the guv'nor, for the plump one smiled her into a dark hallway. The contrast between the inside of the factory and the waiting-room was staggering. Adah waited a little to get her eyes used to the darkness. There were no windows at all in the narrow hall. At the end of the hall were dark matching stairs. There was no lino or carpeting of any sort on the dark stairs.

'Go up, turn left on the fourth landing and the door with "Manager" on it is the guv'nor's'. The plump girl did not wait for Adah to thank her but disappeared quickly. Adah was unsure whether it was worth pursuing or not, but since she had got that far, there was no point in her turning back. She might as well go in to see what it would be like to work as a char in this prison-like factory.

Her tap on the Manager's door was feeble and gentle. She half hoped the Manager would not hear her. At least that would give her more time to brace herself. Bad luck. The Manager heard all right and invited her in.

Yes, she could start work the following day . . . something, something, something . . . she was too nervous to listen properly.

'Now your pay,' said the guv'nor. He seemed to have an almost triangular face, the upper part of which was wide, with cheeks slanting gradually away until they finished in a sharp and pointed chin. The chin stood out at what looked like a good ninety degrees. His mouth was small with surprisingly full lips. He had little hair, but what was left of it was black with lots of grey. He blinked frequently as if he had sand in his eyes.

Adah set her large eyes to work, the man relaxed and smiled but the smile was too genuine, too proper, for a char. She was dressed like a hippy. She had on a pair of blue cotton jeans and a big pair of boots she had collected from the clothes exchange. Round her neck she wore a couple of blue bead necklaces which she had bought from a bargain stall at the Crescent the week before. She knew that she had to look and behave in a casual way. Not that she would find it difficult to be accepted as a cleaner because her skin colour was always an asset in such cases – a qualification almost. It was never thought to be below any black girl to want to char. That was usually her role until things started to change. But the man with the triangular face saw through her.

'What are you studying?' he asked, forgetting that he was supposed to be telling Adah something about her pay.

'Well, I'm not really a student as such,' she drawled, hating the man's curiosity. Why couldn't he just employ her and have done with it? Why did she have to explain to this man that she was a student, a mother of five, dreaming that one day she would become a writer but for that moment, living on the dole and at the famous Pussy Cat Mansions?

The man was patient, waiting. Adah explained, but made sure she left out certain convenient facts. She did not tell the man that she had five children; she did not know why, but felt that her role as a mother would not be welcomed. She did not tell the man of her dreams to be a writer, but she did tell him that she was reading for a degree in Social Science, part-time. She gave him the impression that she was sure to fail because she thought that would make him happy. Not many old-timers can stand young and boastful young people – even white ones.

His look at Adah was piercing, searching. She twisted her hands and moistened her dry lips. Why must people want to know so much just for the sake of employing a cleaner?

The man decided that she would do. He went on weighing her up as he talked and Adah had the uneasy feeling that the man thought she was lying. He spoke.

'The woman who was doing this job was in her fifties. She had to leave because her feet started playing the poor woman up.'

Adah was not surprised at this. With those Godforsaken stairs, anything could happen to a middle-aged woman. She felt sorry for her.

'We used to pay her six pounds a week; how about that?'

That would have been more than right for her, but she knew that The Law would not allow her to earn that much. The Manager looked like someone who would ask her to get an insurance card. He definitely did not own the factory. The Social Security would cut her allowance if she earned anything over two pounds and she would be worse off after what was obviously going to be damned hard work. The Manager did not ask her how she made her living, otherwise he would have refused to employ her. But Adah wanted Christmas presents for her kids. So she told one lie.

'I have a grant for my studies, and I'm not allowed to earn more than two pounds.'

The Manager's lower lip hung low. 'We can't share the work into two. You should have told me that before. I don't see how it's going to work.'

'Oh, no!' cried Adah jumping from her seat. 'It will work. I'll make it work. I'll do the work, you pay me only two pounds. Honestly, I *need* that extra two pounds.'

The Manager's eyes shot open like bright stars. 'You mean you'll take two pounds for a six-pound job? You must be out of your mind!'

'No, please, sir, I'm not out of my mind. It's just that I need the money very badly.' She waited to see the effect of her outburst on him. She again set her eyes to work. But she had to work them harder on this horrid man to get her way. He was still doubtful.

'I've never come across or heard of a cleaner like you before. Have you done any cleaning job before? No? So you see, you don't know what you are letting yourself in for. It's research, isn't it? You want to do some research of some sort, here in our factory?'

Adah was angry. All this fuss just for a cleaner's job. She did not care any more. The man was as narrow as his narrow face. He's acting like a manager, she thought, though she did not really know any managers or anything about them.

'I'm doing no research. I only need this money to buy Christmas presents for people I love. Of course after Christmas, if the atmosphere here is all right with me, I shall go on working. After all I'm doing you a favour, I'll be saving your company four whole pounds a week. You should be begging me to stay.'

Even if the man was not a mean person he behaved like one. He was mollified. He guessed that Adah was telling him the truth. 'Well, if you want it you can have it, but to me it looks like exploitation. We'll make it up for you though. You'll be given some luncheon vouchers, and instead of working from eight to one o'clock, you can always leave at twelve. You'll work it out for yourself, and find the places that must be cleaned every day. And every Friday, if you want, I shall take you out to lunch.'

He gave Adah a twinkle with his bright eyes at the last statement. Poor old fool; he thought Adah as a typical case of an easy conquest. 'You know the trouble with you, you should marry a rich man.' The Manager had a sense of humour, all right.

Adah brightened and thanked him. She started work the very next day. In less than a month she was able to buy a toy sewing-machine for her oldest little girl, some nice painting books for the younger children and a pair of rubber gloves for herself.

The factory men were not bad. What amused her were the girls working on the factory floor, who kept talking down to her just because she was only a char. She was beginning to see herself as another Monica Dickens or that jolly Margaret Powell who wrote *Below Stairs*. The Manager was no longer mean to her. He gave her food vouchers, gift vouchers, endless tips for nothing, but Adah knew he was trying to make up the difference in pay. Invariably he would tell her not to worry with his office, because it was too clean. Adah was grateful.

But the work was telling on her in other ways. Even before that Christmas, she was behind in her work at the school; she could not submit any essay at the end of term. When she came back from her work at twelve-thirty, she always fell asleep in the afternoon. Many a time she would be woken up by her children. She would even be too tired to welcome them properly. The Manager was right – charring *was* a tiring job. She just managed to drag herself to her classes in the evenings, thinking often of the old lady with the bad legs, who, unlike her, would probably have been taken for granted.

All of a sudden, or so it seemed, she began to cough. She started to dread climbing those stairs – at first she had thought it would do her figure some good and made light of them. Suddenly she remembered Carol. She went to her and told her the story of her job.

Carol could not believe her ears. 'You're working yourself to death. Something has to be done.'

Carol was true to her promise. She wheedled and wrangled and somehow Adah was given a grant of two pounds a week, for ten whole weeks. She used the money to cover the expenses of the winter peak period. Meanwhile her cold developed.

She was frightened of going to her doctor. She was such a large and impersonal 'science' female who had a way of making everybody feel that she was your doctor, your Female God. With one sweep of her cold eyes she could reduce any orator, however confident, into an incomprehensible fool. Adah coughed all night, her temperature rose. All she wanted to do was to sleep, and that sleep was the sleep of the near dead. Food tasted funny, and she could not eat.

Then fear gripped her. *Suppose I should die, what will become of my children?* They would take them to a home, maybe. And then . . . and then they would grow to become delinquent coloured youths who would not know how to love, because they had grown up without any. *Please God, I pray. You can't kill me now. My little girl wants to be a children's doctor, the boy a space scientist, my other daughter simply wants to be a mum, with loads and loads of children, while the second boy wants to be a policeman, a gambler and a doctor all at once; the baby is too young to want to be anything. Well, all I want to give them is a good home background with warmth to cushion them through life*. After a good warm home with lots of love, any child would surely have enough confidence to be anything. Not just to be anything, but make a success in whatever he or she decided to do; even gambling. After all, is not the whole of life a funny sort of gamble?

She muddled through the morning housework somehow, and sent a note through Titi to Carol. 'I'm dying,' she said in the note. 'Please come, I want to make my Will.' She laughed at her own awful sense of humour. Her Will indeed! What had she got to will to anybody? A pair of shoes each for the girls when they reached the age of twenty-one. The boys could sell the sewing maching and share the money – but she had not finished paying for it. Well, she was not really dying now. The good God wouldn't let her. He could do without the like of her for some eighty years or so.

'Why, what's the matter with you?' shouted Carol, her bulk shutting off the light from the open doorway. 'Your eyes are so red.'

'Well, I er . . .' the long and painful cough intervened. Her chest wheezed, tears flowed from her eyes, and she made an attempt to laugh, so that Carol might think her brave.

Unfortunately Carol did not think it was funny. That woman had no sense of humour. She took things rather too seriously.

'Go to bed and stay there,' she commanded with her sergeant-major voice. 'I must get a home-help. Who is your doctor? She must come here at once. You should have called her long before this. Just stay in bed and no more nonsense.'

Adah crawled into bed, not to rest but to worry. Call that doctor into a flat in this condition! The floor had not been swept for two days. Kids' litter cluttered every corner. She was not sure the windows were all opened. Then she remembered that it was still winter. But she was sure there must be a wet bed upstairs. She wished she had been white and middle-class for then there would have been no need to worry – the doctor would have 'quite understood'.

85

As always, it was confidence that she lacked. She wondered where people learned it. From childhood she supposed – well, she had never really had any childhood. That doctor would be angry at being dragged out of her surgery in weather like this.

Adah did not know what happened after that. She drifted into sleep.

'You must stop that bleeding job.' It was Carol's voice. Authoritative. She had no bedside manner. She had even acquired some of the Pussy Cat's adjectives. Long associations tend to make us what we are. Did Byron say that? Carol marched out to get a home-help.

Whoopey was better than a million home-helps.

'I didn't see you out this morning, so I came to ask what the matter was. Are you hiding a fancy man in your bleeding flat? What are you hiding for? My! Adah, you do look ill, though. Honest, you look very ill. You should have sent your little girl to tell me mum and me. Your eyes are like fire.' Whoopey rattled on. She pushed Adah back to bed. She dashed upstairs to the kids' beds, put the wet things into the wash-tub, played records, smoked endless cigarettes, and watched the telly.

Hours later, two ladies descended from the Children's Department. They were both well-wrapped in long tweed coats with matching hats. Their voices were low and cultured. They cooed and tutted, and were very sympathetic. Their voices squeaked like Whoopey's, but their squeaks were of a different kind. Low, not high-pitched. Just like a hen with young chicks. Their laughs were more strictly relevant – even appropriate. They took Adah's supplementary benefit number and advised her to let the children do more housework. They obviously hadn't listened, or at least understood, when she had explained the ages and she felt too ill and tired to explain all over again that they were much too young to help. Whoopey almost knifed them from the back when they said this. They promised to get a woman to do out her flat for her but 'You must know, my dear,' said the more social of the two, 'these things take time. We have to fill in several forms, and make endless telephone calls, but we'll do our best. Take care of yourself.' They went away feeling very helpful and charitable.

Meanwhile, Adah could hardly hold her aching sides. Whoopey engaged herself in mimicking the two good ladies.

'What fucking housework do they want five- and six-year-olds to do? Oh, blimey, these women, they make me sick, Adah, they do. I want none of them around me when I'm poorly. What do they want you to do in the meantime, while they make their damned calls?'

The big doctor was the next to call. She was precise. 'Take this to the chemist for her,' she commanded Whoopey.

The tablets were very helpful. The first night Adah was delirious. She talked to her mother who had died a long time ago. Her mother stood and chatted with her on their sun-bathed veranda in Lagos. She fought with her boy friend at the street tap, and later they married. She remembered the Shakespearian parts she played at her school dramatic society. She was beside the Australian headmistress she had at school telling her that she was cut out for greater things.

'Wake up, you talk so much in your sleep that my baby can't sleep. Oh, blimey, you talk all them funny languages of yours all the time. 'Ere, take more of this, it will do you good.' Of course, it was Whoopey again, so warm at heart, so simple in her ways, aggressive only to those who treated her as a semi-animal.

No home-help came: none were available because of the bad weather but the office 'was doing everything possible'.

Adah got better but she was weak for several days after her illness. Another type of talk was going round the Mansions, which frightened Adah more than her recent 'flu. The Council was going to move everybody, so said the news. She should have been happy, since they were going to move into a new and cleaner environment. But she was still unsure of herself.

She was a regular reader of *New Society*, and some other social science magazines. She was not unaware of a few social theories. But the situation that was working itself out at the

87

Pussy Cat Mansions fitted into no such theories. As a sort of community had worked itself into being, everybody knew the business of everybody else. That sort of life suited her. There was always a friend to run to in time of trouble. It was like living in a prison. Prisoners, after a long stay, usually find outside life more demanding. She was known at her local library, she now looked on school as an extension of her family and the fact that her children were on free dinners no longer worried her. The headmistress had said to her once, 'I do lose my temper when your sons look bored, because I happen to know the standard you expect of them.' She was one of these people who had come to regard her as a human being caught up in uncomfortable circumstances. To go to a new area now seemed as formidable as going to a new country. Most tenants at the Pussy felt differently; they looked forward to the change. They had their relatives living nearby, so they did not have to depend on community life like Adah. The 'good' families did not like to be called 'problem families', a term which seemed to stick to any family living at the Pussy. Some of the Pussy sons were already being called skinheads. This enraged many mums. Hair was easier to keep clean when it was cut short, they did not want youths that were Jesus-haired.

There was a Christmas party at Carol's. The children were loaded with more gifts and goodies. Adah did not go to the party, for it was on one of those occasions when she felt fed up with being given things. She felt her dignity as a human being was being gradually taken away from her. After all, they would move some time in the New Year so she might as well start learning to live by herself, making her own decisions.

On Christmas Day, she and her kids went to the church. It was extremely cold, yet the vicar was exceptionally inspired. His sermon dragged on and on. Bubu's version of the Christmas carol was a joy to listen to.

'Oh, come, let us annoy Him,

Oh, come let us annoy Him, Christ the Lord.'

The bigger children shivered uncomfortably in their new clothes which Adah had bought through a mail-order catalogue.

After church, they ran home. There was a small Sainsbury's turkey in the oven. She had held back the rent for a week to buy that, and she also bought a small bag of coalite, just to give the living-room a festive air. The kids had never seen so much food. They ate sweet corn, sausages, turkey, and what Adah said was Christmas pudding. Her kids refused the latter, though. They preferred the ones they had at school. Adah did not blame them because she had never seen any food look so ugly.

They were lucky that Christmas. Many of her old African friends paid visits, and they paid indirectly for the food Adah gave them with money. The money she kept to repay what she had 'borrowed' from the rent. She kept the turkey for a week – she kept slicing and re-heating it until there was nothing left but the bare bones.

She gave away many of the boxes of chocolates which were given to her. She gave a box of giant After Eight mints to the nurses at the nursery where her youngest went. She gave an assorted box of biscuits to the library assistants at her local branch. That, she was sure, would take care of overdue charges for the following year. She would always be sure to get most of her college special text books reserved for her. She did not like the large amount of overdue charges she had had to pay in the past year.

That Christmas was a white one. After the hullabaloo of the week before, the great day was deadly quiet. It gave her the impression that Christmas was only celebrated in shops. There was so much rushing and hurrying, so much spending and giving, that, to Adah, Christmas ended on Christmas Eve.

As usual, all the things people rushed to buy the night before become unwanted litter on Christmas Day. On their way back from church, Adah and her children saw Christmas wrappers and crackers all gaily dotting the otherwise flawlessly white snow. A few children were being pushed out in the snow by enthusiastic parents to show off their gleaming prams, bicycles, and giant dolls that did everything. Some of the parents stood by the door admiring their children. It was unfortunately too cold for much talk.

Towards the evening, more snow fell, obliterating the footmarks made in the morning by the few people who had ventured out. Inside Adah's flat, there was warmth and laughter. Her children were already getting bored with their new toys. The doll's cot which was the baby's had been dislocated. She came to Adah, tears in her eyes, and commanded Mum to 'fix it'. Adah was trying and retrying this, finding it difficult to know which part belonged to which, when she heard Mrs Cox, croaking what Adah later found out to be a Christmas carol. The baby momentarily forgot her unmendable 'dolly cot' and listened, sucking her fingers thoughtfully.

Adah knew that Mrs Cox was trying to knock at her door. She was either too drunk to do it properly, or too cold to know what she was doing, for she was banging at Adah's toilet window instead. She lumbered in when the door was opened, with a bottle of cheap red wine under her arm. Whoopey soon joined them, and a Christmas party was in full swing. More sweets and chocolates were pressed on the children. Unfortunately neither the feeders nor the fed knew when to stop.

They all sang carols until they were hoarse. Many of them they sang out of tune but, as Mrs Cox said, God would forgive them being miserable offenders. She assured everyone that she still remembered what it used to be like in the churches. She knew how Christ was born. And she knew what it was all about. She would not say it before the children though, she assured Whoopey and Adah. Before long, her songs were not only out of tune, but scarcely came out at all and then only drowsily. Christmas itself was coming to an end.

The bottle of wine had long gone, so had Adah's Emva Cream Sherry. She too was becoming sleepy. They were woken by one of Whoopey's children. The poor boy was doubled up in pain. 'Ooh, Mummy,' he screamed. 'My tummy, it hurts, Mummy, oh, Mum.' The mums suddenly became wide awake. Mrs Cox blamed her daughter for giving the children too much chocolate.

'You brought the lot, Mum, you did,' snapped Whoopey as she made a dive for her little boy while Mrs Cox still sat, too drunk to get up.

'Not too bad for the last Christmas in this place,' put in Adah. 'This time next year we'll probably be somewhere else.'

'I shan't miss this place, God knows,' said Mrs Cox, as she heaved her bulk from the couch.

'Adah, come here. Bubu has been sick all over the floor,' called Whoopey.

Adah dashed into the corridor and saw Bubu in a mess. Whoopey hurried her two green children out. The air outside was bitingly cold. They all shivered involuntarily when Whoopey opened the door to go out.

The unprepared Christmas party had been a success. Adah cleared up the sick. Life at the Pussy, like that Christmas, was always spontaneous. Nothing was planned, everything was done as it came, naturally. Adah was no longer sure whether she would feel at home in places like the British Museum or the big libraries where she used to work. In those places, your laugh was regulated, intellectual, artificial. No spontaneity. You waited for others to finish what they were saying before you made your own contribution. You seldom listened to what the other person was saying, and by the time it came to your turn to speak, your point would no longer be relevant. You would have forgotten what you were going to say anyway.

Adah shivered as she mopped and disinfected her corridor. Outside, there was going to be a blizzard. More snow fell, and there was hardly a ghost in the street. The end of another Christmas.

12 *The Ditch-Dwellers' Revolt*

Christmas went, but the cold lingered. Everybody's spirits, after they had been given their temporary boost by the Christmas rush, sank back to normal with the weather. Snow fell heavily in the compound and the 'juju man's' little house in the centre looked like the habitation of the angels, all clothed in silvery white. Pussy Cat Mansions, when covered with snow, was good enough for a Christmas card – the type of Chrismas card seldom seen these days. Those traditional cards looked heavenly when seen in Africa; Adah remembered that they used to give her a sort of purifying sense. The modern cards seemed to jeer at Jesus, with reds and yellows splashed about the cards like children's art. It is modern art of course, but people like her found it difficult to interpret. She was happier with what had already been interpreted for art illiterates like herself. Pussy Cat Mansions in coats of white would gladden the heart of any artist, modern or traditional.

Inside the flats it was another story. People felt cut-off, as, indeed, many of the old people were. Kids could not go to school for their free dinners. They slipped in the snow, and most of the teachers were at home sick. Adah would have stayed in bed to read, but her kids seemed always hungry and demanding constant feeding. They wanted freedom to run about, even though there were paraffin stoves about and these kept her on her feet all day, rescuing or guarding. The sitting-room was warm, with layers and layers of wet nappies dangling and dripping before the fireguard. The social officer had brought the fireguard to her a few days before, after wringing her hands for weeks over the fact that Adah was still heating with paraffin heaters.

Frustration combined with helplessness and anger came over her. Suddenly she felt lonely. She did not feel like complaining or moaning to anyone. In any case, no one at the Pussy could have given her the sort of help she needed. Her supply of food was always low, and with the kids away from school the food ran shorter still. Because of Christmas, most mothers on the dole had been paid two weeks in advance. That meant that they would have to do without pay. She was a week in arrears with the rent. Tired of being alone with the children, she decided to pay the Coxes a visit.

'Where are you going, Mum?' asked her watchful children. They saw their mother getting out her red spotted scarf. Whenever Mum fetched that scarf, it meant outings. The kids never missed a thing.

'I am only going to Whoopey next door,' she replied, knotting the scarf under her chin.

'Can I come too?' Dada begged.

'Oh, no, you'll only wet your pants there, and that could start a smell.'

'No, Mum, my pants are dry,' and she lifted up her dress for Mummy's inspection, standing astride for her to have a closer look. Dada's eyes were eloquently hopeful, her head was turned to one side.

'No, I shan't be long,' Adah said, as she dashed out of the flat. Dada's screams were deafening.

At Mrs Cox's everybody was feeling as low as Adah, but unlike Adah, they had found a scapegoat. The fact that they had suffered too frequent doses of disillusionment, coupled with the humiliation of seeing their pride as human beings constantly questioned, found an outlet in their anger against 'them', particularly against Carol.

'Damn Carol,' Whoopey spat. 'She tells them everything

about us at the Town 'all. Blast her. We must move from these bleeding flats. We must make it clear at the meeting tonight. We must all go, you must come too, Adah.'

'Is Carol not on our side? She should come with us, don't you think?' Adah asked, refusing to believe that Carol would ever be against them at the Pussy.

'Coming with us? What bloody nonsense you talk, Adah. Didn't you know, if we all move from here, we'll no longer be 'problems'? That means she'll 'ave no fucking job to do. Maybe she'll go back and be just a social officer. She doesn't bloody want us to move.' Mrs Cox panted as she dug Adah's ribs, rather too frequently. 'If we're independent, happy, *she's* out of bleeding work, see?'

Adah frowned. She hated the idea of being used. *Was* Carol using them? Could Mrs Cox be right? But surely Carol was nice. She would do anything, everything, for the poor at the Pussy. Was she really doing all that just so that she would feel needed? Perhaps she was lonely too. At the Pussy Cat Mansions, she was the centre of things. To see her car parked every morning in the middle of the compound gave a great measure of reassurance to Adah and her like. Good though Carol was, where would she be able to exercise her admittedly benevolent power if deprived of the Mansions? Perhaps the Coxes *were* right. Perhaps Carol was trying too much to spoonfeed adults who could take care of themselves.

'What's more,' put in Peggy, Whoopey's sister, 'she has her favourites. The O'Briens. Why should that bloody man stay at home and not go out to work? Why should they live on the dole, and Carol getting them lots and lots of grants from the Children's Department?'

Everybody listened to Peggy because she was an unusually quiet girl. She was in her twenties, and plump as her mother, but unlike her, seldom smiled. Her face was round, fat, serious, just bun-like. She always looked so unhappy. She'd just had a baby, a coloured baby. The result of her last summer holiday. Her voice when she spoke was desperate, violent, and determined. One thing was apparent, thought Adah, this young woman did not like the situation she found herself in. Unlike Whoopey she was never going to accept that situation from society. She would fight to pull herself out of the ditch. Adah learned a lesson from her. She too, would like to face her own world.

But she would still like to be on friendly terms with Carol. She had been spoonfed for so long that she could not cut off from Carol and the Children's Department just like that. The position she was in reminded her of young nations seeking independence. When they got their independence, they found that it was a dangerous toy. She would eat her cake and have it. She would support the move, but must be friendly with 'them'.

'Do you know what the tinkers are?' Mrs Cox asked, cutting sharply into Adah's thoughts. As she did not know, Mrs Cox went on to explain that Mrs O'Brien was one of the tinkers. That was why she was without shame. 'She would cry and tell all sorts of pathetic stories in order to get a few pounds off Carol.'

Obviously, the O'Brien woman was too frank to some of her 'friends'. Adah was scared. She too had recently had a grant from Carol to ferry her through winter. She wondered whether the Coxes knew. Had she been labelled as one of Carol's favourites too? She agreed to attend the meeting. She would have preferred not to get involved, but she knew that the general reaction would be, 'Who the hell does she think she is?' This could make life difficult for herself and her children. She did not wish to be talked about.

The meeting took place at seven o'clock in Carol's office, ironically. The small woman who was the secretary was very articulate, forcefully dynamic, with a limitless capacity for talk.

'Carol calls us problem families,' complained one of the high-ups of the Mansions. 'I never go to her office for anything. She talks openly about people, and your secrets become known to everybody.'

95

'If she repeats what I told her about myself to anybody else, I shall kill her,' Mrs Cox thundered.

The intensity of the whole atmosphere frightened Adah. Everybody seemed to have been wronged somehow. Poor Carol – she was employed to help people at the Pussy, and she did her work well. But somewhere along the line she had betrayed people's trust, or so the people thought. Was the fault really Carol's or that of the bureaucratic institutions she represented? Carol was a fine woman. Many liked her as a person, but few could be sure how much of a real friend she was and how far she was 'The Law'.

'I don't go to her for anything,' said Mrs Williams. 'I really don't like all those busybody social officers. Most of them are unmarried idiots and know nothing about children. As soon as they put on a white Godforsaken raincoat, they think they can dictate to you how you ought to live.'

All Carol's regulars were quiet; even Mrs Cox was silently chain-smoking.

Adah made a great effort to explain. 'We are not all problem families, you know.'

'Yes,' agreed the first lady in a green coat, 'but why do they always call us that? When you go to them fucking clinics you tell them your address and they say you are a problem. I want to move out of this damned place.'

Mrs Williams, a West Indian, stood up, shook her big brown hand in the air, 'I am an honest-to-goodness hardworking person, not a bleeding problem family. *They* have problems, people who go about nosing into other people's business. When they grow old, who is going to look after them when they have no children of their own?' (A typical West Indian-cum-African ideology, Adah thought: you have children who look after you when you are old.)

'When they grow old,' she went on warmly, 'they go to those damned old people's homes. I don't want that sort of old age for myself. That should be their problem. They are problem people too, for no woman is happy without kids of her own. They should solve their own problems first.'

'One of them,' the woman in green rejoined, 'one of them came to me the other day, when I had two babies in the bath, the other two children had only vests on and they ran to open the door. The woman talked to me for a while over this and that, and then left. Later, she wrote to the school to say that I needed help because my children looked deprived when she called. I could kill her. The school gave us some clothes which I gave straight back to the teacher.'

'Yes,' thought Adah, 'these things do happen. Why do certain people feel it right to put labels on others? A brown person is labelled "black". A poor family is labelled "problem". A lad who decides to wear his hair long is called a "long-haired layabout". Another boy who decides to wear his hair short is labelled a "skinhead"; a traditionalist is "square" and a modern thinker is "Bohemian". The world is beautiful, but its inhabitants create problems for themselves.'

When Adah had left work months before, she had begged for a nursery place for her kids, so that she could have the whole day free to do her studies at the Senate House. Her appeal was refused by Dr Somebody from the Children's Department on the grounds that she was not gainfully employed. An unnecessary problem was created for her by that doctor. Luckily the nursery matron was kind and motherly and knew why Adah wanted her children in the nursery. On that very day, the social officer for the whole area had paid a visit to the nursery complaining: 'I seem to have run out of problem families. The working classes in this area seem to be problem free.'

'Oh, no,' shouted the matron. 'Go to number X of the Pussy, there are lots of problems there.' The social officer came and listened to Adah's story; consequently her kids were retained at the nursery. This took three weeks of clerical work and several visits to her by different social officers. So Adah knew that sometimes they could create problems. She noticed that one was encouraged to complain and whine, otherwise one would never be noticed. At the Pussy, the greatest whiner got the greatest attention. Many women in her position did not know what their entitlements were, so they felt they must beg. One clerk from the Ministry might recommend five pounds for new curtains, another nineteen. Women of the ditch had to live at the discretion of such men.

A complicated affair had happened not very long before at number Y. The girl involved had two children by her husband, but unfortunately he was put inside. The girl was young and beautiful. She became pregnant again. Rumours had it that she never went to the clinic. Few people were actually sorry for her, for she kept herself to herself. What worried people was how she would live after the birth of the baby, because it was certain that her allowance would be cut off. The girl looked frightened too. Mercifully the child was stillborn in her sitting-room. One could feel the relief that went around. The Ministry did not know of the birth of the baby, so nothing was done to her.

Adah was much surprised when she came across a young female sociologist who was expecting her second child. Both babies were by different fathers. The Ministry maintained her through her confinement until she was strong enough to go back to work. The sociologist had known of and asked for her rights. Women in the ditch were always too ignorant or too frightened to ask for what they were entitled to. People like Carol were employed to let them know their rights, but the trouble was that Carol handed them their rights, as if she was giving out charity.

The arguments at the meeting over definition went on for what seemed ages. Adah made another attempt to define what a problem family was.

'We are not all problem families, you know. A family is a problem one if, first, you're a coloured family sandwiched between two white ones; secondly, if you have more than four children, whatever your income is; thirdly, if you are an unmarried, separated, divorced or widowed mother, with a million pounds in the bank, you are still a problem family and lastly, if you are on the Ministry you are a problem. . . .'

'Rubbish!' shouted Mrs Williams, cutting Adah short. 'I live between two white neighbours, and we get on very well together. Why then should I be a problem just because of that? I work, my husband works, my children go to school, then where is the problem?'

'I have six children and, believe me, we are plain working-class people, and I am no problem to nobody. Blast those women,' shouted another voice from the corner.

The atmosphere became heated, arguments mounted. Carol was torn to shreds, called all sorts of names, and Adah was looked at rather suspiciously. One old man pressed home a point. 'Your friend calls yours a problem family because of your, your – you know, your skin.'

'She asked for it,' said Mrs Williams, defending the old man.

There were open grievances against 'them'. The annoyance was almost tangible. The type that caused the oppressed to revolt. The next subject was how to force 'them' to do 'some'ink now'.

All the mothers were to leave their children for 'them' and make 'them' take the kids into care. Then they'd be forced to 'do some'ink'. The suggestion came from the dynamic lady in green.

It was a good idea, and everybody agreed to it. There was to be a protest march, followed by a long sit-in, in front of the town hall, with crazy banners waving, and as much howling as possible. At the end of the day the kids were to be left at the door, with a letter and all the used banners.

Adah's confidence wavered at leaving her children outside in that cold air. She determined to pay a whole day's visit to the zoo with the children on the day. She stopped attending the meetings. Meanwhile, she was still one of the tenants.

It is funny how one can be easily influenced by a group. Adah started to dwell more and more on those little wrongs Carol and her group of bureaucratic social officers had done to her. Some of the wrongs were real but most were imagined. Many of the genuine wrongs became magnified out of all proportion. She suddenly realised that she had hated the free meals given to them at Christmas. The more she thought about it, the more ashamed she felt. With the new talk going on at the Pussy the shamefulness loomed larger. She was surprised at her behaviour. She was grateful then, but now she did not like it at all. It was wicked to feed people who were not refugees, people who could work and do something for their food. It was wicked to feed them as if in a charitable institute. She agreed with the Pussy dwellers that Carol was not one of them. She was only pretending to be. They were being used for her own self-satisfaction.

The next important event was to be a social one. There was to be a dance in the church hall. Mrs Ashley's daughter who worked in 'an office' was to bring a pop group. Adah was to bring 'coloured men'. No one listened to her when she said repeatedly and truthfully that she had none to bring.

'Don't lie to me,' laughed Mrs Cox. 'You have lots of them. Yes, you do. Bring them nice tall ones.'

Adah knew she would not attend, not because she was a snob, but because she had no nice tall coloured man she could persuade to come with her. She said nothing.

The excitement over the coming event melted the great annoyance against 'them'. Everybody went back to being their happy natural selves. The happiness was heightened by the fact that after the dance the march would follow. Even Adah was beginning to look forward to moving out. She started to yearn for a little privacy. The idea of life being doled out to her became more oppressive as winter gradually gave way to spring. When she moved into her new place she would stay in isolation.

Nobody will know me, I shan't even go to the church. My children won't have to apply for free dinners.

As soon as one allowed one's kids to apply for them, the school social officer would call, then there would be endless

100

forms to fill in and the history of one's failure to keep one's husband would be raked up all over again. No, in their new school, her kids would just pass as ordinary kids.

'Adah, are you going straight back to your flat?'

'Yes, why, Mrs Ashley?'

'Well,' she lowered her voice and eyes, and covered one side of her mouth with her hand. 'Well, you see, Mrs Jaja has done it again.' Mrs Ashley looked very embarrassed. She scratched her million curls, pulled her grey giant muffler higher round her neck.

It was a cold night. They had all been sitting in Carol's office to discuss the final arrangements about the dance. Carol's office had giant electric fires. These, together with the ever-present arguments, heated the meeting place. The cold wind outside struck them like invisible demons when they came out of the meeting place.

Mrs Ashley came nearer to Adah, breathing heavily in gasps. 'Mrs Jaja has left the old man again. She didn't take any of the kids with her, so I'm going there to help put them to bed. Would you like to come? It's still very early.'

'Yes, of course,' answered Adah, without hesitation.

Mr Jaja was an old Nigerian student who had come to England in the forties for further studies. He was a retired Civil Servant from the then Nigerian Civil Service. He had two wives and a large family of children in Nigeria. After he came to England, the diplomas and the degrees did not come as planned. He married again, a white woman who was a drunkard and a jailbird, or so the story went. The woman was young, in her thirties, whereas Papa Jaja was probably in his seventies. He looked seventy, on the wrong side of it too. He had broken black teeth, white hair, dry wrinkled skin, and a mouth that was perpetually wet and dribbling. Every time they ran short of money, the missus disappeared usually for weeks. She was a born complainer and would see faults in everything and everybody, even in God. She had blessed Papa Jaja with six unruly children.

Mrs Jaja had said once to Adah, 'They call my kids coloured.' Her kids were all half-castes and very beautiful they were too.

'Well, call them pinkies and be friends,' Adah replied promptly.

She remembered that weeks before, her son Vicky said that one of the Jaja kids called them blacks. She knew that Mrs Jaja was dissatisfied with her lot, but then who was really satisfied with what life had to offer at the Pussy Mansions?

She and Mrs Ashley went to the home of the Jajas. The amount of filth and disrepair in that flat would frighten the germs. There was no lino or any form of floor covering on the stairs. Most of the floor was bare. The children clutched at what looked like blankets and peeped at Adah and Mrs Ashley. They giggled and shivered as they stood around a low fire watching the ever-present television.

'Now to bed,' ordered Mrs Ashley, throwing her muffler on a table that was already cluttered with broken dolls and other twisted dirty toys. Papa Jaja came out of the kitchen. The strong smell of something sharp filled the room. He came into the room carrying a big bowl of white chips.

'Are you sure that those chips are properly fried?' Mrs Ashley asked, peering into the bowl.

'Yes, they were cooked, not fried,' croaked the tired old papa.

'Well, it's past nine, hurry,' went on Mrs Ashley.

'Don't hurry them, it's only ten to nine.'

The kids swarmed round the bowl and attacked the potatoes with amazing speed.

'Wait, I have to get some salt. I forgot to put some in when I was cooking.' He hurried back into the kitchen to get the can of salt, but he was too slow and the kids were too fast. The chips had disappeared before Papa arrived with the salt. Papa sighed.

'I didn't know that you could cook chips,' said Mrs Ashley tactlessly.

'It is nice,' snapped the biggest boy. He stared at Mrs Ashley and his eyes were challenging and full of hatred. Mrs Ashley shut up. After supper the two women helped to wash the children and brushed their thick bushy hair, which was almost impossible to comb.

'Thank you for coming,' Papa said. 'Why don't you wait and have a cup of tea?' They both refused, but Mrs Ashley accepted a fag. Adah contributed very little to the chit-chat that followed. She was too sorry for those children to be able to say anything. Mrs Ashley had known the family for a long time, and she and Papa Jaja took the situation as normal. The Jaja woman had always been like that.

It looked as if it was going to snow. So they said their goodbyes and 'see yer in the mornings', and the two women went to their different homes. Mr Ashley had already put their two young girls into bed, and the big trendy one that worked in an office was reading a magazine.

Adah's feet were cold. Her kids were in bed already. She woke them all up and made them sit on the potty. Putting them back to bed, she thought of all the day's happenings, each incident a contrast to the others.

She made herself some coffee, filled a hot-water bottle for her cold feet, moved her bed from the weeping wall and slept soundly till morning.

13 *Drifting*

The weather became much milder. The inhabitants of the Mansions had survived another winter. A few of the sophisticated Mansions' aristocrats had put their potted plants out on the balconies. It was constantly wet and mildly cold, but the air was fresh. Excitement started to mount again at the Pussy. Everybody was determined not to spend another winter there.

The proposed march did not take place. Miraculously, Carol came to know everything that was discussed at the ditch-dwellers' meeting. She came to Adah one morning, flustered, and looking worried.

'I'm in such a mess,' she began. 'I'm supposed to have defined to you what a problem family is. You poured out the whole definition to them at your meeting.'

Adah's mouth went dry. In the first place, the discussions they had had at the meetings were supposed to be confidential. In the second place, she had said nothing against Carol. Why should she be the scapegoat? She knew the colour of her skin made her 'scapegoat-able', but she was not going to have it. Martyrs belonged to the Dark Ages and to history.

'Yes, many things were discussed at our meeting. They were not meant for your ears, though. During the discussion I attempted to define what is classically meant by a 'problem family'. I made the attempt to clarify some points, not to slight you. Whatever would I want to do that for?' Her voice started to rise.

'I told them that I had only discussed it with you academically, and they retorted by calling me a nigger lover!'

Now why did Carol say that? Even if they did call her that, should she have told Adah in that mood? Adah felt small at this announcement, but knew that it was quite possible for someone to say a thing like that. After all, the twisted old man did say something like it at the meeting. Both women knew that they would gain nothing by prolonging the matter.

Adah's face must have shown some disappointment, for Carol said, 'Don't worry, I shouldn't have said that.'

To Adah, it was like going back to the melting pot. So people had been sniggering behind her back – a Mrs Know-All. What then should somebody like her do? Avoid people, because they called her names, or resort to violence? *I can never win*, she thought, for she hated violence. *I'll just have to learn to live with it and do nothing.*

Since Carol knew of their secrets, the Town Hall must know too.

Adah was sewing when she heard the clip-clap of her rusty letter-box. She was not expecting anything important, so she did not bother to see what it was. Tired of sewing, she was beginning to pack up when she heard another loud bang on her door. She could not possibly ignore this; it was too loud, too determined. She peeped through the letter-box to see the Princess standing there.

'Did you see the bleeding le'er?' she shot at her when she opened the door. The day was so exceptionally damp that Adah had placed a cylindrical oil-heater in the hallway to dry off a bit of the wet before the return of the kids. The paraffin smelt heavily, but she was used to it. The Princess was a delicate woman and chesty. She coughed out her words. Adah could not invite her in because of the smell. She thought it would just be too wicked to ask her in.

'That must be the letter,' she said, picking up a white folded paper from the floor. 'What is it about?'

The Princess cupped her flabby fleshless breasts in her

palms and coughed, a long, whining and painful cough. She was impatient too, worsening the whole cough. She wanted to tell Adah what it was about before she could read it for herself. Unfortunately the cough prevented her from doing this. Before she could collect herself together, Adah had read the essence of the letter. There was to be a 'conference' of the tenants and the councillors at Haverstock School.

'That's great,' Adah said, happy.

'Great! They want to silence us, that's what. The Tories 'ave took over this area, so they'll never listen to us. We must have our protest march.'

'Who told them in the first place? That's what I'd like to know.'

'I can't tell you that, but don't you know?' whispered the Princess.

'I know that fat cow did. There is no other person who would.'

Everybody got excited about the conference. At the wash-house down the road, Mrs Williams and Mrs King practised and repractised how they were going to talk to the councillors.

'My bath has been blocked for months, you know. I must tell him that,' stated Mrs Williams.

'I really don't want any repairs. I wrote to the Prime Minister about my broken windows the other day,' Mrs King volunteered.

'Yes, you did, didn't you? What did he say?'

'I don't think he replied to the letter himself. It was typed. Very large typing it was. He said he had appointed some local somebody to do the job. He said he was very sorry about the broken windows.'

'That must be very exciting,' said Adah.

'He didn't write the letter himself I be . . . Charlie, Charlie, come here, there's no flipping soap in this damned machine,' Mrs King shouted.

Charlie was a surly, slow, fat, easy-going man. Charlie never hurried. He had worked at the wash-house for years. He knew these women, and they in turn knew him very well. His work was to look after the machines, and to keep an eye on women who cheated, or those who could not bear to share with others.

'What's the matter with the machine?' he asked as he wound his way through mums, kids, tables and bags of washing.

'No soap in number eight,' Mrs King declared.

'Well, you know, don't you, that you've put too much in it.'

'I did not,' shouted Mrs King, looking aggressive.

Charlie knew better. He moved slowly and pregnantly to the back of the giant washing-machine and pressed a knob. Soap bubbled into the machine and Mrs King was gratified. 'Ta, luv, have a fag.'

Charlie had the fag lit for him and moved away majestically to another screaming woman by the rolling machine. Her best bath towel was stuck in it. She was screaming the place down, but Charlie took his time.

'I'll miss this place when we move,' Adah volunteered, as the scream died down, giving way to the general hum of the washing-machines and the occasional shrieking voices of tired women. 'It's so cheap,' went on Adah. 'All twenty-eight pounds for only five bob and no need to buy soap.'

'Well,' said Mrs Williams, 'my sister moved to one of them high-up places, near Mornington Crescent. She still comes to the wash-house once a week.'

'That's interesting, how does she do it?'

'She puts her wash in an old suitcase and comes up on the bus.'

'Go away and play in the front room, and leave me apron alone,' Mrs King digressed as her little boy started to dip his hands into her apron pockets, probably for some pennies. 'That would be very difficult though,' she replied, after having successfully shooed away her little boy. 'I can't see myself doing that, it would be too much work. Still, we can't have it both ways, can we?'

'No, we can't,' agreed Adah, while she mentally calculated the cost of coming from Mornington Crescent to Prince of

Wales Road just to wash clothes. It would cost at least two shillings more, to say nothing of the strain of travelling with a heavy case.

'Charlie, this washing is not clean,' she said, showing an old grey bed sheet to the other women and to Charlie, who happened to be passing by. She knew though that no amount of washing either with the ordinary soap or the new biological miracle soap would restore its whiteness. But with her neighbours watching she would like to blame the machine for her grey results.

'You should have said that before the machine stopped,' Charlie pointed out to her, as he moved nearer to Adah's washing. His pale bloated face accused her. The man had long eyelashes. Wasted on a man who worked in a wash-house, she thought.

'Next time, you tell me before it finishes.'

'Yes, Charlie,' Adah agreed quickly. She re-dumped the soaking washing into the gaping hole of the machine. Charlie restarted the machine and the other watching women, knowing that Adah would go home with a very clean wash, cooed.

Mrs King could not keep her feelings to herself. 'Nice that's nice.' The envy in her voice was eloquently loud. The machine leapt into action and Charlie went away.

'He's ever such a nice man.'

'Yea, that's what I always say to me husband. I always say to 'im, "Charlie has the patience of an angel." '

But the question was, had Charlie any choice? To argue with an overworked mum, hurrying to get 'Bob' from school, was like remonstrating with the moon. The moon would even be better, because at least it looks bright. But not these women. Charlie's long experience had turned him into an 'angel'.

At the rolling machine the other two women, Mrs Williams and Mrs King, were ready before Adah, because Charlie had given her a 'second go' at the washing-machine. She packed her dry washing into an old carry-cot and excused her way between women in different stages of relaxation. Some were having their cuppas, other fat ones were busy stuffing buns into their ever-willing mouths, and making efforts to talk at the same time. Adah kept shouting, 'Excuse me, please.' Of course many were too busy to hear. She gave a gentle push to a rather big woman who stuck her posterior out in a disturbing way. She swung round, rather too quickly for her bulk.

'I am sorry I poked your bottom,' Adah apologised quickly.

'You did what?' said the woman with the offending bottom. 'Oh, God, did you hear her? You're a rotter, aren't yer? . . . Go on,' and she gave Adah's bottom a gentle kick, almost losing her balance in the attempt.

'Serves yer right,' another onlooker contributed.

The old lady at the roller sniffed as Adah approached her. She spread her bed sheet wide so that Adah would not have a place to do her ironing.

'Would you move to one side, lovey?' Adah begged, uncertain. 'You can make room for me if you fold your sheet double. Sheets come out better when they're done that way,' she finished brightly, feeling helpful.

'Wait, I've almost finished,' declared the old lady, stationing her little old body at the centre of the roller so that Adah would not have any room at all. Adah, a regular at the wash-house, knew all the tricks. She said no more, but acted. She took her smalls, particularly the baby's smallest pants, and pushed her way, wordlessly, but with resolution, to the machine and started with the shabbiest of the pants. She put them determinedly on top of the old woman's snow-white and over-pampered sheets.

'Oh,' she protested, 'you can't tell me not to finish me sheets, can yer?'

'No, darling, I can't tell you that, but I can tell you one thing – this machine takes three people, not one.'

'Take those old things off me sheets, do you hear?' the old lady shrieked, her voice shaking.

'I can't take them off, dear, they're already in the machine.'

'I don't understand you people, really I don't.'

'That's bad, love, but have you ever wanted to understand?'
'Wotcha talking about?'

'Never mind, love. Here comes your sheet with my old things on top of it. You may have to wash them again.' Adah was determined not to spare the woman's feelings. She sometimes got really fed up with being treated as semi-human.

The lady hummed, stamped, and banged things about, and Adah hummed a pop song. The old lady lowered her voice and spat out spitefully, 'Why don't you go back to your own bleeding country?'

Adah had sensed that the old woman was going to say something like that. She was also aware that other mums were listening, interested. So she raised her voice and said, 'You don't look English to me.' It was a wild guess. But her long stay in England had taught her that the really happy balanced English natives were the least obstructive to immigrants. The old woman's hair, though liberally sprinkled with white, was too black for her to be real Anglo-Saxon, or whoever the original people were.

'She's a Greek,' yelled Mrs Williams from the other roller. Everybody laughed.

'Shut up, you black savage, you never even wear pants in your own country.' The old lady's daughter materialised from somewhere.

'Have you any pants on yourself?' Mrs Williams wanted to know, her arms akimbo.

'Yes, I damned well *have*,' shouted the young woman, quite carried away. She lifted the edge of her skirt up. This brought a gust of unexpected laughter from the watching women.

'She thinks we're in Soho,' Mrs Williams said.

Charlie came in, saw the situation and advised the old lady to learn to give and take. She was too flustered to continue her ironing. She packed her things, including the unironed ones, and went home, her daughter following.

Two other women joined Adah, and they shared the machine without any argument, and Adah as usual started to

110

blame herself. She should have let the old woman finish. She should not have allowed Mrs Williams to ridicule the young girl; she should not have used the woman's own weapons by accusing her of being an immigrant. But didn't the woman go out of her way to be nasty to her? She did not feel happy about her going away and not having her washing properly done. There was nothing she could do about it. Mrs Williams was already talking about something else.

Their walk home was short. They all went to the school to collect the kids and the whole noisy bunch stopped at the sweet shop for lollies and sweets. Bubu's nose was running as thick as melting candle wax. Adah bought a toilet roll and cleaned his nose with it. It was better to buy a toilet roll for such things; tissues were softer, but dearer.

'You must come very early to the meeting tonight,' Mrs King said, as she jostled her kids into her flat. She lived on the ground floor.

Adah, with the help of her kids, worked her way up the wet stony stairs.

'I've joined a gang today,' announced Vicky, Adah's biggest boy. He was five.

'Have you?' asked Adah, as she puffed her way up the never-ending stairs. 'What does your gang do?'

'Kiss chase,' he answered promptly.

'Kiss what? What does that mean? Don't you go and start anything funny at your age. What does "kiss chase" mean, huh?'

'Well,' expanded Vicky, happy to get the attention he had been craving for. 'It only means, Mum, it's not bad at all, we chase the girls and kiss them and they laugh all over the playground. And you see, Mum, I've got a girl friend too.' Vicky's face was a picture. His eyes dilated, and his face glowed. To him he had walked on the moon. 'I'm going to marry her.'

This last statement was a warning. Adah could not condemn him. He was a highly imaginative child and did not always know where dreams ended and reality began. Adah smiled but said nothing.

Inside the flat, they started to unpack the washing. Then Titi asked, 'What's your girl friend's name?'

'Alison.'

'That's a nice name. Is she white or black?'

'Oh, I am not sure. She's both, I fink.' The boy looked puzzled. 'You see, she has curly hair, and she is a girl.'

'You're a stinker. You don't even know if your girl friend is white or black. You're daft, you are.' Titi was really annoyed at her younger brother.

'You don't know everything, you know,' defended Vicky. 'Anyway, I'll ask her tomorrow.'

Adah looked at her son. It was funny how kids could be so colour blind. Absentmindedly she cuddled the sweat-soaked curly head of her little boy. *In a while the world will teach you what colour your girl friend is. Before even you kiss chase her you'll think of her colour first.* Vicky looked embarrassed and shook himself free. One did 'kiss chase' with one's girl friend, not one's mum, his reproachful look seemed to say. He was unused to such an affectionate demonstration from his over-worked mother. 'I am big now, Mum,' he warned.

'Yes, darling, I can see you're very big.'

Adah was late for the meeting. The big hall was packed and a councillor was talking. He would do this and this and that and all those. Every tenant would be moved by June. It was a blow to Adah. And the new councillor sounded as if he meant it. Adah was forced to pay attention. Everything was happening rather quickly. O God, help me, she prayed. To move from the Pussy Cat Mansions to the new City Match-Boxes was out of the frying-pan into the fire. At least there was warmth at the Mansions.

After the meeting, Carol invited Mrs Cox, Adah and Whoopey for coffee.

'You're getting fat, Adah,' observed Whoopey. 'You shouldn't be drinking that.'

'You think I don't know, but it's the chance of a lifetime. It's not every day that you get invited for a creamy coffee in front of the Round House.'

'Oh, leave her alone,' Carol said, watching Adah spooning the cream into her large mouth greedily, and with so much noise and clatter. She licked her lips with such a smack that the others laughed.

'I can see that you are enjoying it,' Carol said laughing.

'Delicious,' said Adah. She was amusing them and she knew it. For how else could she accept bought food from another woman, knowing quite well that she would never be in the position to pay her back. She had to amuse Carol, but the funniest thing was that while showing her gratitude in that way, she was really enjoying herself too. It pays sometimes not to take the world too seriously. She was very full.

'Let's go to the pub,' suggested Whoopey. Drink was Whoopey's speciality.

They went into the pub just in front of the Round House. The noise and heat were almost unbearable. A few people were sitting but most of them were standing and swaying dreamily to the sound of music. Most of the women were dressed in modern gipsy fashion and wore beads and bells. The clothes had no definite pattern as such – just anything. Even African designs were rampant. Adah had never seen so large a group dressed so trendily in such a small place. The language, too, was different. One person came to Adah, his arms went quickly round her waist. She did not know what to do, so she helloed to the person. 'Sweet dreams,' said the individual. Adah was uneasy, as she could not tell whether it was a he or a she. The face was shaped beautifully but the drape on the head was like that of a male Moslem. She looked round for Carol and Whoopey and was not surprised to see them being kissed alternately by a man with a beard, long enough for Jesus of Nazareth.

'Sweet dreams,' repeated Adah's companion. It must be a sort of salutation, so she 'sweet dreamt' back to him. This person had no beard, and Adah had the uneasy feeling that she was being cuddled by a woman.

They started to dance. The dance was a sort of drift. One drifted to and fro to the sound of music which was almost drowned by the din. She luckily caught Carol's eye and told her she would like to go home. Carol agreed, for her male companion probably found it much easier to hold Whoopey by the waist than Carol.

'Aw, must you go now?' sweetly complained Carol's former partner. 'That's a shame. Just as I was beginning to know her. Isn't she a sweety?'

Mrs Cox came to the rescue just in time, pulled her tipsy daughter away, collected up the packets of fags being given to her by the new lover-boy as the man swayed to Adah's former partner. She was now sure she had been dancing with a woman. She felt cold all of a sudden.

A week later, the moving business was beginning to be real. Her next-door neighbours, the classy ones, were one of the first families to be moved. They were very happy to be going away from the ditch because the son of the family worked. The mother was once a widow, living in the ditch with the other women, but her son had now pulled her out of it. Their family was complete. The Smalls did not need any community to make them happy. They had formed their own.

14   *The Mansions' Ghost*

In a little less than two months after the meeting at Haverstock Hill, the Mansions were almost empty. Most of the people had gone, leaving the dregs — those who owed enormous rent, or those who had never had the courage to ask to be moved. Adah was one of the latter group.

'This place smells awfully bad,' Whoopey breathed one day as she was balancing her two children up the stairs.

'Yes, and dark too; do you know the caretaker puts the light out at nine, so coming up the stairs at night I'm ever so frightened,' Adah said, sighing.

'Yes, I am too. Know what? They don't bother about us no more, you see they don't want to waste money on us no more. Have you got an offer yet?'

'No, I've not even been to the office since the meeting,' Adah explained.

'I thought as much, because you are not in arrears, are you?'

'No, I'm not, I just don't know who to go to. I'm not really too keen.'

'Well, listen,' advised Whoopey, 'everybody must leave this place. No one is going to be left behind. So you better make up your mind where you're going. I haven't got a place either, so we can go to Mr Persial tonight. He's the one you ought to see. He fixes everybody. He'll fix us all right.'

'I remember him, the nice one who came to see us the other

115

day. But he promised to write to me soon,' Adah said, frowning in concentration.

'Well, he'll never do that until you go and remind him. We'll go together, I'll leave me kids with me mum, then we'll go. I had an offer, but didn't like it, only two bedrooms. I want three bedrooms – two for the kids and one for me.'

'Perhaps they want you to share a bedroom with the baby.'

'I think so, but what happens when he grows up? 'He's eighteen months old now, and where does my fancy man sleep when he visits me. That's why I want to live away from me mum, you see. She's a born nosey parker.'

Adah and Whoopey involuntarily looked over the balcony into the compound. A group of about six or seven people were gathered in front of Number X. It was one of the single-room flats occupied by the very old. There was a council van waiting outside the flat, and two men who looked like ambulance men. They were talking excitedly and knocking at the old lady's front door. There did not seem to be any reply from the flat. Whoopey and Adah watched absentmindedly.

'Don't you go about with fancy men, now that you're going to be alone by yourself, Whoopey. Why don't you take up something, sewing, painting, oh, anything to occupy your time, now that your family will be separated from you?'

'Yea, I'm thinking about it too. My sister is taking up nursing. She wants to stay with Mum, so that she can mind her kids while in training. She wants to start making her own clothes too, like you do.'

'That will be nice, though,' commented Adah, her eyes still fixed at the goings-on at the old lady's flat on the ground floor.

'Look, Adah,' Whoopey gasped, 'they're breaking down the old woman's door. Look here, I think she's had a stroke. Let's go and see.'

They ran down. Adah picked up one of Whoopey's kids. The little girl protested loudly, but Adah held her tight. When they got down, they ran to the old woman's door. The two men in uniform had apparently brought the old lady's 'meal on wheels' for her. The story was obvious. She was dead – had probably died in the middle of the night or that very morning. Nobody would be able to say for sure. Surprisingly, her untouched milk was still by her door in a half-pint carton.

Whoopey and Adah did not go in when the men eventually forced the door open. 'Poor Mrs Jackson, she was such a nice old thing,' Whoopey mourned. 'Do you know, Adah, a little while ago, she could have been buried here?' Whoopey pointed to the cemented ground in front of Mrs Jackson's flat.

Adah's gaze followed her direction. She read the 'In Memoriam' to someone with a shudder. Pussy Cat Mansions was built on a cemetery. She shuddered. Oh God!

'Whoopey, we *must* go today to see Mr Persial, I must move from this place.'

'So must I,' said Mrs Ashley, who was standing by. 'I have had an offer though, but they are doing the place over. It's terrible to die like that with nobody around to make it easier. It's them damp walls that killed her. It's wicked to let the old people live in a place like this.'

'I'm sure she died in her sleep,' Adah consoled.

She and Whoopey were so preoccupied with the goings on that they only answered Mrs Ashley's nervous remarks with monosyllables. But they were suddenly woken by Whoopey's boy who, finding himself free and bored stiff with just standing there, dashed into the old lady's flat. Whoopey made an accurate dive for him and fished him out by the hair. The boy was smacked, and the two mothers went upstairs thoughtfully. What a terrible life for a lonely woman, thought Adah *O God, let me die in my country when my time comes. At least there'll be people to hold my hand.* But then her thoughts went to her people who had recently died in the bush during the Biafran War. Most of them had died from snake bites, running away to save their lives. There was no safety anywhere, really. One never knew. Suppose she died in the sea, the air or anywhere where there would be no bed at all. She told herself not to be stupid, that she was still young, and that death was still a long, long way off. She liked to think that death was only for the old and tired ones. Mrs Jackson's death had shaken her.

Mr Persial's was next door to a hippy dwelling, or what looked like a Simonian shrine. The house was splashed with hideous blues and bloody reds. His room was awful. It was meant to be a temporary office converted to meet the emergency house re-allocation. The chairs were all stiffly lined up like a classroom. All were worn and shabby, probably left by some tenants who were grateful for leaving their old and damp houses for new and more modern ones. The floor was unswept.

When Whoopey and Adah came in, Mr Persial was talking to a plump blonde woman about her rebate. He talked in a calm cool way, exuding confidence.

'Of course, everything possible will be done in no time at all. You must not worry. You'll definitely get your rebate. These things take time, you know, but don't worry. I'll see what I can do about it. Tomorrow in fact.' The woman was pacified, but looked cynical as she thanked Mr Persial and walked out.

'This is Adah,' announced Whoopey. 'She has had no offer and she wants four bedrooms and you'd better give her a new property because she's cleaner than me.'

Mr Persial smiled. He was a bald man with puffy eyes and a lazy smile. He looked Adah over pleasantly. He took his pen from the shabby desk and poised it in the air. His smile became broader, including Whoopey in a rather indulgent way. He fished for a form and Adah supplied the details.

'But look, Mr Persial, I'd like a house. A converted house with central heating. I won't mind the age of the house as long as it's private and with four bedrooms,' Adah added hopefully.

'I'm sorry, we seldom have houses with central heating and four-bedroom flats are rather difficult to get these days,' replied Mr Persial.

'All right. What about a four-bedroom maisonette?' Whoopey asked.

'I can't promise, but I'll see what we can do.' Mr Persial must be finding the phrase 'what we can do' rather handy. Reminded one of the clerks at the labour exchange.

'Make sure you give her a new property,' said Whoopey still adamant.

'As I said, we shall see what we can do as things turn out. There are three-bedroom maisonettes all over the place, but four . . . well, I can't promise. Why won't you let your baby sleep with you, Mrs Obi?'

Whoopey's flash eyelashes fluttered angrily. Adah shook in an effort to control her mounting fear. What did this man think he was doing? Wanting to push her from a four-bedroom maisonette into a three-bedroom one? She would have none of it. She would stay at the Mansions till she got what she wanted.

'Thank you very much, but the school thinks it's better for kids to sleep away from their parents,' Whoopey's voice squeaked with an emotional crack. 'And, mind you, Mr Persial, that's why you have to get me another flat. I can't share the same room with my son. It's unhealthy,' Whoopey finished, sounding academic, quoting the social officers.

Mr Persial refused to commit himself, but he was amused. Whoopey and Adah looked determined. They would not leave the Pussy until they'd got what they wanted. Mr Persial was saved from the verbal onslaught that would have followed by the entrance of two other women. The two new women seemed to give him a certain kind of courage. They were impatient for Whoopey and Adah to leave and Mr Persial had the impression that Whoopey would not be too insulting while the two new arrivals were watching. Mr Persial therefore took the opportunity to lecture the two Pussy Cat tenants on the subject of large families.

'Trouble is, large families are not trendy any more. Families are smaller these days. We in England don't have large families. We now reduce the number of our children because it's more economical. In fact in most civilised societies that's the new unwritten law.'

Whoopey got lost in the maze of the argument. She did not

care so much about civilised societies and unwritten law. But Adah felt that Mr Persial was accusing her personally. He nailed the last nail into the coffin by saying, 'You must have loved children, or been careless, or both.'

Adah's self-control left her. Who was that blasted clerk who thought he could tell her what was right and what was wrong? 'Would you, sir, consider the Kennedys uncivilised or untrendy? What do you think of the Royal Family? Who is going to replace all those thousands of children being killed in Africa by some woolly-headed political idealists? Tell me! You dare sit there and preach to me about the world's population explosion in a place like England. Why don't you go and preach your sermon in China and Japan?' Adah was carried away, but Mr Persial got the message.

'I am sorry I annoyed you, madam. I did not accuse you personally. I was only trying to explain to you why it is impossible to get you a four-bedroom flat at the moment. Most of the flats are designed for smaller families. But, I assure you, you'll be hearing from us soon.'

That was one of the things which still baffled Adah. The Englishman. The educated ones would make anything feel important, as long as that thing was a woman. An African male would have marched her out. After all, she was begging.

Two days later, she had an offer, and she went to view it. It was a new flat, maisonette of some sort, and on the fourteenth and fifteenth floors of an ultra modern sky-scraper. One of the new wonders of modern London. Inside was new, clean and very bright, but when she looked out from one of the sitting-room windows, she saw the ground dancing before her eyes. She shut the window very quickly. It took her time to recover from the giddiness. She did not want the place but was doubtful what the reaction of the council officers would be. She locked the door and walked out. She'd rather face them than live day in and day out at such a height.

'Hello, hello, Bubu's mum.' Adah spun round and saw the mother of one of Bubu's classmates smiling her greetings.

'Oh, hello, so you live here?' asked Adah, surprised. 'It's new. I didn't know you lived here.'

'Oh, God,' moaned the young woman. 'This is where we live.' She ran her hands through her unbrushed hair, scratched her head a bit, then wrinkled her smooth face. She looked tired. Unhappy. 'We came here three months ago, but Jesus, it's awful. The height's enough to drive you round the bend. I'm so frightened. Are you coming to live here? Don't take it. Whatever do they want you to do with all your kids when the lifts break down? It has broken down about six times since we came here. I leave everything to John to carry up for me. It's killing. I have to stay by the kids all the time, see? If one should fall out, he or she would be ground to powder. It's so far from the ground. I don't like it at all. We are leaving soon. It's no good for folks with young kids. I daren't have another child in this place.' The woman probably hadn't seen a soul to talk to since her John left for work.

She went on, 'We are halfway nearer God in a place like this.'

'So we would have made half the journey when our time comes to save God the full fare,' Adah quipped, trying to cheer her up.

'Yes, that's what I've always said too, but we have to wait until we die. What's the point of being halfway there already when we are supposed to be still alive? Mind you, I am halfway there already, and believe me, I shall be there soon if we stay long in this space. The doctor has put me on sedatives. It's so unreal. Don't accept it, and don't tell them I told you.'

'Thank you,' said Adah thoughtfully. 'I don't mind the height as long as I don't look out of the windows, but the thought of the lift breaking down and my having to carry my baby, push-chair and shopping up fourteen floors! Huh! What happens when I leave the children all alone in the flat to do my shopping? I'll go mad with worry. I shan't be able to do the shopping properly.'

'Well, I'll tell you something,' confided the woman, 'when we moved in here, we thought I'd have to do some part-time job, cleaning, you know, in the mornings for say a year, to pay for the furniture for this place, but I'll tell you one thing, John is so scared the kids might fall down and break their little necks. So you see, we can't even make the place look nice. John earns so little, you see. It all gets me down.'

'I am not accepting it,' Adah said finally, her mind made up. She pushed her chin forward, and smacked her lips noisily. A determined attitude of hers.

'That's the best decision you've ever made in your whole life, I can tell you. And you know something? If you accept it, they'll take months and months to move you out if you ever change your mind about the place. You wouldn't like that, would you?'

'I can't even face another move, when I think what this is going to cost me. I'm on my own, you know, so you see I can scarcely manage at all.'

'Listen, dear, you're better off. My sister is on her own, and she gets all the help she needs with the kids, free dinners, free tokens and all. Them welfare people visit her and give her bags of money and gifts. Her flat was furnished for her by the Security people. You see, if you're married you don't get any help at all. Mind you, John is good, though, and I wouldn't change him for anything under the sun, but when I come to think of it, it's all wrong some'ow. Why should I be poor because I'm married?'

Yes, it was all wrong. Mrs King at the Pussy Cat Mansions pushed her husband out because she was better off without him. She was happier being on the dole and as a separated mum. She even bragged about it. 'I'm on me own, you know.' That was the only way she could keep herself and her children decently clothed. The children would be better off with one happy relaxed parent than two harassed and unhappy ones. No child grows into a normal adult in an atmosphere of hate. Very few animals can survive without some measure of relaxed love and security. But here this woman was trapped by the love she had for her John. Mrs O'Brien of the Pussy solved her own problem by making her husband stay at home with her. She in fact was having her cake and eating it. She had a loving husband, a helper, and enough money to keep them above the poverty line, even enough to spare on the Bingo. Rumour had it that he sneaked out to work somewhere without getting a card. But it paid them to live that way.

Everything is so unfair, Adah thought, as she handed the forms back to the Housing Department. The young lady clerk in a swinging skirt wanted to know why Adah did not accept the offer. There was too much to explain, so Adah put on her studied African look, shut her lips, and would say nothing. That was very easy to achieve because she had a tight scarf over her head knotted determinedly under her chin. Her face was shiny and unmade-up, her lips tightly shut. She reserved such looks for places where she knew society expected her to look poor.

'Don't you understand English?' the girl clerk demanded, exasperated.

'No, no, no want that 'ouse. No want,' Adah replied, shaking her head like a toothless baby. She walked out quickly, still shaking her head. She did not want to be recognised by Carol and her friends.

The girl simply stamped and stared. 'These people, these people,' she said, shaking her head too.

Two other offers came after the skyscraper offer. One was to share a house with an old woman with a dog as big as an elephant. The dog barked so savagely that for a moment Adah was sure it had been trained to butcher all blacks on sight. She did not even have the courage to open the door. She wondered how such an old woman could manage such a mighty creature. After the last offer which did not appear to her suitable, she decided to stay put. She would stay at the Pussy Cat Mansions. They would have to do the rebuilding around her. She was afraid of facing a new and demanding situation.

Tired of being by herself in such an uncertain state, she paid a visit to Carol's office. All the regulars were there. Many who had moved away had come from their new homes to rake through the left-over pieces of furniture and old things which Carol was getting in plenty from the Salvation Army. The Princess looked very nervy, unsure and unhappy.

'I've moved out now,' she informed Adah. 'I moved yesterday. It's centrally heated, and easy to clean, and it's dry. I like it.'

'Good for you,' Adah enthused. 'What floor are you on?'

'The first and the second. They put me there because of my feet. I can't climb stairs. It's very nice of them.'

'Now,' put in Carol who was trying to phone someone, despite the din. 'What do you want me to ask them for, Princess?'

'Yes, thank you, I need mats for the bathrooms. The floors are cold without bathmats.'

'Hello, hello,' bellowed Carol unhappily. Everyone could sense that Carol was indeed very unhappy. It was apparent. The loud jolly Carol was drifting away with the Pussy dwellers. She would lose her Pussy sheep, because many who moved away from the Mansions were determined not to be problem families any longer. She might have another community though, if she was lucky. But meanwhile her dependants at the Pussy were all moving away, and for Carol that was a worrying thought. 'Look here,' she thundered at the telephone. 'These people have nothing. Bathmats may be cheap to you as a salaried officer . . . All right, all right, I shall fill in the form for bathmats, but see that you attend to it quickly. Princess suffers terribly from sore feet.' She banged the phone down. The sound died slowly, and everyone was quiet, ashamed somehow. They felt that they were using Carol for their own ends. Carol was tired.

'Thank you,' the Princess said, trying to break the ice.

'I do wish you'd stop thanking me, and I want you to know that I'm not your social officer any more. I'm handing you over to your new social officer. I am no longer your officer, right from the moment you move from here.'

This was a truthful announcement, and all the women in the ditch knew it. But to have it thrown at them like that was painful. It seemed as if Carol was saying, 'If you refuse to be problem families, then you're no longer my responsibility' – and no longer her friends. Did Carol want them to stay there in the ditch, so that she could always have people to brag about as her 'cases'?

Adah had been humiliated by Carol in this way several times. She had told Carol a lot of things as her Family Adviser, but Carol had a way of babbling her stories to her friends, and worst of all, when Adah was there. In most cases she would ask Adah to confirm the story and Adah, not wanting to do without a grant which Carol might get her, would retell the story. The pet story that amused her friends most was the story which Adah had jokingly told Carol about her inability to start her coalite fire the first time she had attempted it. Carol had repeated it so many times, and to her face, that Adah knew at one time Carol always took her to such parties and gatherings as one would take a joke. But Adah knew that she would have the last laugh. She would tell such stories only when she was sure there would be a grant coming. This sort of affair had been undercover. Mrs O'Brien had her own method, that of bursting into tears and making Carol feel like a deity dispensing charity. Carol had liked all these roles; now she wondered how she would be able to find again a group of people who would be prepared to be humiliated, whose secrets could be made public jokes, while keeping quiet about all Carol's little weaknesses?

Only the day before, Whoopey had expostulated to Adah that they were being used, and that she, for one, would never go to one of Carol's lousy gatherings. 'She only goes there to make a show of us,' was Whoopey's cruel verdict.

Looking at Carol after her outburst, Adah suddenly felt cold. She realised that she was shivering. She had allowed Carol and her other social police to use her more than she had intended to. It was never too late to be wise. They had all been reduced to this state of apathy, inadequacy and incompetence. It was

125

painful, but there was nothing they could do. Some of the women reacted violently.

'You don't have to tell her like that, you fat cow. Let's go away from this bleeding hole,' exploded Mrs Cox.

'As soon as they move you, she doesn't care about you any more,' whined the Princess, piteously. She was actually crying.

Everybody started to shift towards the door. The feeling that those left at the Mansions had overstayed their welcome was apparent to everyone.

Carol was mollified, embarrassed to realise that she had been wrong in exposing her feelings. What she did not know was that everybody knew of them but was too scared to say for fear of losing the 'Carol bounty'.

'Please, Adah, *do* wait a minute,' she called in a tired voice.

Adah was sorry for her. She had thought that Carol made jokes at her expense and to her face because she was a black beggar; she did not know that that was her habit in dealing with all her 'cases', both white and black.

When the room was empty, she said to Adah, 'They worried the Council into moving them out of this place. I don't know why they still cling to me. The senior officers at the Big Department think that I like to work with all of you all the time.'

That was a dilemma, Adah thought. It was probably difficult for Carol to part with them. Why did she not break down and cry, and let people know she cared? After all, whether she made jokes about Adah or not, Adah would always remember her as a friend who made living in the ditch bearable, though she would remember her kindness in her own way. 'When I move, I'll avoid you as much as I can,' she decided. 'You are a kind person, but until you stop talking down to your fellow human beings, you'll find it difficult to get loyal friends, and your kindness will come to nothing.'

'Have you had an offer yet?' Carol inquired.

I have not had a suitable offer, but I'm sure that I shall soon get what I want.'

126

Carol smiled, a wan and noncommittal sort of smile. 'I shall always keep in touch with our Adah.'

Adah swore at herself for not seeing the goodness in this woman. Perhaps she was lonely and very vulnerable, and more sensitive too. She was, after all, human, and tolerating the 'little ways' of women in the ditch could not always have been easy.

Adah, not knowing what else to say, thanked her and left the office. Her walk back was slow and meditative. The Mansions were ghostly in appearance. Uncleared rubbish heaped from chutes into the compound. *I suppose I have to go. I have to be out of the ditch sometime, I have to learn to make my own decisions without running to Carol. I may or may not have any social officer any more. When I'm in need, I can always write to them. It does not pay to use somebody else as a means to an end.* She thought she had been using Carol to get easy money, but in the process, she realised that Carol had been using her too. They were both at fault. No malice. No offence. But one thing about which she was determined was that she was not going to lower herself any more for anything. The world had a habit of accepting the way you rated yourself. The last place in which she was going to incarcerate herself was in the ditch.

She walked rapidly towards her flat, but stopped to read for the last time the names of those buried at the Mansions cemetery. 'Goodbye, ghosts, whoever you are, and sleep well.'

A group of the ditch women stood by the door that used to belong to the Princess, silent, looking lost. Adah did not feel like talking, so she went inside her flat.

On the brown, damp mat behind her door was another envelope. Another offer. She would accept it.

A week later, she moved out of the Mansions, away from the ditch, to face the world alone, without the cushioning comfort of Mrs Cox, without the master-minding of Carol. It was time she became an individual.

127

15 *Into the Match-Boxes*

Adah liked her new maisonette flat very much indeed. She occupied two whole floors and central heating was installed. She was drunk with joy over the district, just in front of the famous Regent's Park. It smelt of money and real wealth. Her own working-class council estate was cheek by jowl with expensive houses and flats belonging to successful writers and actors. This was very frightening at first, especially as there did not seem to be a street market like the Crescent she had been used to for years. She was yet to discover Inverness Street and even this was a long way to go to shop for a family of six, with a baby to push or carry.

Opposite her window was a shop selling antiques. From this she learned that there were different kinds of old furniture, some of it in the shop apparently worth several hundred pounds. Next to the antique shop was another with expensive pianos. Well, she had been dreaming of living in a middle-class neighbourhood and now she'd got one. She was determined to enjoy her new surroundings.

Her first difficulty was shopping. There was not a single bargain shop near her, so she knew that she would be paying regular visits to the Crescent. This would mean money for fares. She'd have to manage somehow.

The flats were built rather like a child's arrangement of match-boxes. In flats like those, you couldn't holler to your neighbours in the mornings when you were hanging the babies' nappies out to dry. In fact, sometimes you got the feeling that you were a Robinson Crusoe, all by yourself. The walls were dead, completely sound-proof so that the flats were peaceful and private but with this came the isolation which is the debit side of privacy. There was no compound like the one at the Mansions; instead there was a narrow corridor all white, like a hospital, lined with white gleaming Flash-washed doors. Each door panel had its own number plate.

The match-box flat was beautiful. Outside, the whole block looked like a model factory, all solid, full of wide glassy windows and very white doors.

Loneliness descended on her during the very first week she moved in. She did not know a single one of her neighbours, so introductions were out of the question. Everybody was 'new', and newness has a very peculiar effect on people. Nearly all the tenants were playing at being big. The flats themselves were brand new and most of the occupants had come from worse surroundings. Adah, too, decided to join in playing big. It was high time she should, she told herself.

On one of her weekly visits to the Crescent, she walked into Whoopey. Whoopey looked very shabby to her. Was she beginning to let herself go, perhaps because she never left the Crescent area? Or was it that Adah was now used to seeing well-dressed men and women in her new place and saw Whoopey with fresh eyes? She did not know which, but what she did know was that she and her children had stopped wearing clothes from the clothes exchange; there was no clothes exchange in Regent's Park. She had improved her sewing and started making things for herself and the kids. At least these things were new and clean though some of them were not very smart.

'Hello, Mrs Queen,' Whoopey called to Adah. 'You dress like the queen of our Crescent. Have you come into a fortune, or did you win the pools? My, you look different. You've changed a lot.' Whoopey was beginning to shout in her excitement.

Adah too was excited, and she embraced Whoopey like a sister.

'You look different too, Whoopey, but, Jesus, I am very happy to see you. Your kids, are they all right?'

'Yes, they're all right. You know some'ink, Terry is at school in the nursery class. Susan is starting next term.'

'Good for you, so you have all your time to yourself now, though I must say *I* find that away from the Mansions and with no Carol, time just drags and drags. I have no one to talk to except the kids. It is nice but lonely in the match-boxes.'

'Yer. I know,' agreed Whoopey. 'It's even worse for me, because this is the first time I'm living away from me mum. I miss her though she visits us several times in the week, still, I miss her.'

'I wouldn't like to go back to the Mansions, though. I like it where I am now. It *is* expensive and lonely, but I still like it better than the Mansions.'

'People do get used to new places quickly, I suppose.'

Shoppers pushed and jostled them as they stood there and talked. All of a sudden, Whoopey asked Adah if she had noticed any difference in her. Adah, tactfully avoiding the subject of her dress, replied that she had not.

'Look closely, daftie,' Whoopey commanded. Adah still did not get what it was Whoopey was trying to tell her.

'I can see that you are dying to tell me something. Please do, I'm very bad at solving riddles.'

'It's no riddle,' Whoopey laughed. 'It's only that I've met him, only last week, I realised that I fell the very month we left the Mansions. I am so glad about it and I'm sure the bloke will ask me to marry him soon.'

'Oh, Whoopey, I'm so happy for you. But this bloke, how did you meet him so soon and when is he going to marry you?' Adah knew that she was asking dangerous questions which she had no right to ask. But she was shocked at the news that Whoopey had not learned her lesson and that there would be yet another baby for Mum to worry about. As soon as she had rid herself of her family, she fell. Still, she could not tell Whoopey how to live her life.

'The bloke is one of your people. He came here to study and he's in a flat next to mine. I had to know him, you see. One night I ran out of matches, and I went to knock at his door. He gave me a big box of matches and since then we've become very good friends.'

Adah simply gaped, not knowing what to make of this story. She knew her people. The man was probably just lonely, like Whoopey, but to seriously consider marriage with a girl with two children was out of the question. How could she tell Whoopey that she would get hurt? What help could she give? There was nothing she could do but just keep nodding and wishing Whoopey luck. Whoopey was so certain about this bloke that Adah could not bear to ruin or dampen her joy. Instead she changed the conversation. 'What did your mother say?'

'I've not told her, but I saw Carol yesterday and I told her. She was happy for me. Very pleased she was. The bloke, his name is Jako, has lots of books, a big radiogram and television with BBC2. He likes kids, so in the evening we all go to his flat to watch the programmes. The kids love it. When he finishes his reading he's going to be the accountant for your whole people.'

Adah did not doubt Whoopey's faith, though she knew in her bones that she would be hurt in the end. But why deprive her of a little happiness, however short-lived it might be?

The day was a Saturday. Saturday was always busy at the Crescent. There were many Indian shops selling African food, and this drew large numbers of Africans into the Crescent Market. The market was once in the centre of a poor working-class area. But modern housing estates had sprung up round it like mushrooms; people got mixed, the rich and the poor, and there was no knowing which was which.

The noise, clatter and bustle was like that of birds in an aviary. People screamed and tumbled into each other, arguing and protesting over rising prices, filling the air with their shouted communications. Children with chocolatey mouths and fingers followed the trails of mums with shopping trolleys loaded to overflowing with 'bargain' foodstuffs. Africans, Pakistanis and West Indians shopped side by side with the successful Jews, Americans and English from Highgate, Hampstead, Swiss Cottage and other equally expensive places.

Another of her old neighbours, Mrs Cook, came up from behind; she was Jamaican. Mrs Cook stopped short on seeing Whoopey. 'Are you settling all right?' she asked by way of greeting as she moved closer, separating herself from the sea of faceless people.

Yes, thank you, and you?' asked Whoopey absently. Adah turned round to see who it was.

'Oh, it's you,' Mrs Cook said. 'And how is *your* new place?' She wanted to find out, but was obviously in too much of a hurry to want to wait for an answer. She sensed that Adah was going to say that she liked her new flat, so she continued, 'I didn't like mine. We are moving away very soon, next week in fact. We're moving to Holloway Road.'

'But why to Holloway, do you like it better there?' Adah inquired; her curiosity was aroused and she was involuntarily frowning disapproval. 'Moving from one flat to another can be so expensive. It will take me over a year to recover from my removal expenses. Why should they make you move twice in such a short time?'

Mrs Cook sensed that the conversation was going to be more than a mere exchange of greetings, so she put down her shopping, heaved a sigh, and said, 'Well, you see, when we moved they said they were giving us a house that would cost us only six pounds a week, so we decided to take it even though it was almost double the amount we were paying at the Mansions. I went back to work so as to be able to pay for the extra. Later, my dear, they sent us another form, and we've filled it in. You know how much they asked us to pay a week?

132

Well, they asked us to pay nine pounds! Nine pounds a week! That would mean that we would have to pay more in rent than what seven of us would have to spend on food. It was not worth it. Seeing all the flipping trouble we took at the Mansions, we are back to where we started, aren't we? We've found a two-room flat in Holloway Road for four pounds; the building isn't new, but we can manage all right. The children will sleep in one room and my husband and I will sleep in the other. We cook in the hallway. It's not bad. After all, this is not our country, and I don't want to spend all my earnings here. Else, what will I have to take home to my old folks in Jamaica?'

'Did the Council get you this new place?' Adah asked, after a pause.

'No, we decided to do without them. We got it on our own. They can only help people with money, not people like us.'

Adah understood, nodding her sympathy, and Whoopey gaped, unable to grasp Mrs Cook's motives.

'I do wish we could get back to the Mansions,' Mrs Cook sighed, as she picked up her basket of vegetables. 'We are going to live in Holloway for a long time. Please take care of yourself and the kids.' She bustled off, her unbuttoned brown coat flapping away into the crowd.

'She's stupid,' judged Whoopey. 'Why give up a whole house for two rooms just to save a few quid? I'll never do a thing like that, letting five children of both sexes sleep together in one room. I know they are still very young, all under ten, but still they won't grow up properly.' Whoopey knew a thing or two. She liked money as much as anybody else, but she loved it for what it could buy, not just for its own sake.

Adah agreed with both women for she knew Whoopey did not realise that Mrs Cook would be saving a whole five pounds a week by living in Holloway. Five pounds a week added up to a lot of savings.

'I don't understand it,' Whoopey went on heatedly. 'Why deprive yourself of living just because you're saving for the future? If you live well now, there might be some future for you!' Whoopey's voice shook, she was becoming very emotionally involved; her pregnancy was having its psychological effect and she was almost ready to burst into tears. Adah, alarmed, tried to console her, reminding her that the decision was Mrs Cook's own, and since it was her life, Whoopey should not worry too much. Mrs Cook was probably happier with the knowledge that she was saving a lot of money.

The weather was just fine, cool and not too windy, the right type of weather for a good long gossip.

'That's why I like Jako,' Whoopey was saying. 'He lives in a one-room flat all by himself; you know, one of those new types of flats with a separate kitchen. And you know some'ink, if he asked me to come to his country, I'd certainly go with him.' Whoopey rambled on with her usual feckless optimism, and Adah not wanting to deflate her, found herself agreeing, while under her breath she cursed some African men for treating women the way they do.

The doors of the pub opposite them were thrown open. A group of white and black regulars straggled out. One spat. Another glared at the two gossiping women. The dark ones argued with rough-haired friends. There was something extra-masculine about the men, their roughness perhaps. The smell from the pub was both urinal and alcoholic and the Ladies and Gents in the roadway opposite did nothing to lessen the lavatorial stink.

'Hello, sister,' said one of the black men to Adah. She laughingly hello-ed back. She had learned from experience never to rebuff men of her own race; they were more sensitive than others. Even the road sweepers would invariably greet her and she would answer back with a nice 'Hello, brother'. She was not sure why she had this attitude in England; at home she would have ignored them but here she felt that a black man working by the side of the road or in the company of white friends needed to have his morale boosted. Whoopey asked if

134

she knew the men before and she said no. Whoopey frowned and bit her lips, puzzled.

'You must come and see me sometimes,' Adah invited.

'Yes, I'd like to do that, but you're always out, aren't yer?'